The Boys' Life Book of

# WORLD WAR II STORIES

*Each of these exciting stories presents a vivid picture of men in combat—men fighting in PT boats, in tanks, in planes, in foxholes—pursuing the enemy in the deserts of Africa, in the Pacific, in Europe. Some were brave, some were scared, but all of them were involved in the gruelling job of fighting a war that took many lives and changed the lives of people all over the world.*

# The BOYS' LIFE Book of

# WORLD WAR II STORIES

Selected by the Editors of BOYS' LIFE

**Illustrated by Leonard Slonevsky**

*Random House*

*New York*

Acknowledgments

The publishers wish to thank the following for permission to use these stories which have appeared in Boys' Life magazine, copyright, 1943, 1944, 1946, © 1959 by Boy Scouts of America: William MacMillan for Pacific Convoy, Brigadier General Edwin H. Randle for The Coward, Hugh B. Cave for Worth Fighting For, Boys' Life for Desert Raiders and The Chromium Ladder by John B. Stanley and Give it to Them Gently by Richards Bennett. The Publishers also wish to thank The Sterling Lord Agency for permission to use Blitzkrieg, copyright, © 1963 by John R. Tunis, which appeared in Boys' Life in 1963, and The John Day Company, Inc. for The Lost Company, copyright 1954 by The Curtis Publishing Company, reprinted from Combat Stories of World War II and Korea, copyright, © 1962, by William Chamberlain and Hard-luck Regiment, copyright, © 1958 by The Curtis Publishing Company, reprinted from More Combat Stories of World War II and Korea, copyright, © 1964 by William Chamberlain.

# CONTENTS

The Boys' Life Book of
# WORLD
# WAR II
# STORIES

# PACIFIC CONVOY
## by William MacMillan

Though Butch Barclay, the carrier's newest and youngest flyer, stood rigidly at attention while the choleric air officer raked him fore and aft, he was calling himself mentally all the hard names he could think of. Bent on showing the ship's personnel that he was the big shot of the new Fighter Squadron Number Three, he had come in that morning like a bat out of the desert, and all but decapitated the furious signal officer in a crazy power dive to the flight deck.

A roaring in his ears, Butch saw his squadron leader, Red Towner, lean forward and whisper something. Shaking his head impatiently the AO went on in acid tones.

"We have no place on this ship for a grandstander."

"Sorry, sir," stammered Butch, "I—I didn't think."

"That's the trouble with you young smart alecs," barked the commander, "you just don't think. Well, you're grounded till further orders."

Butch felt his world tumbling about him like a house of cards, for he had come to the carrier brimming over with enthusiasm. He stumbled blindly along the passage leading to his quarters. Before he could close the door of the little cubicle that served as a cabin, the squadron leader's big shoulders blocked the opening.

"Tough luck, Barclay, on your first day."

Butch blinked hard. "I—I guess it was coming to me," he said.

The lieutenant's grin was friendly and sympathetic. "Don't hold it against the commander, son. He had to do his duty. Sit tight," he added, turning away, "and maybe you will get the chance to show him that you can do something in the air besides the rhumba."

Ashamed to face the rest of the squadron, Butch kept to his quarters that evening and tried, without success, to figure out why he should suddenly have gone haywire and gummed things up with a silly exhibition of trick flying.

Things kept going around and around in his head without making much sense. And finally, feeling stifled toward morning, he straightened his crumpled uniform and made his way to the flight deck. A dull

moon hung low in the sky and the wind was crisp and
cool. Slumping against the rail he breathed in great
lungfuls of the salty air and looked about him. The
convoy, half a hundred merchantmen of assorted ton-
nage, dotted the sea in orderly lines. Smoke plumed
from their funnels and soapy foam curled from their
blunt prows. It was comforting to know that they
were laden with sorely needed war material supplied
by loyal workmen back home. But the thing that
really impressed Butch was the three rakish looking
destroyers hovering protectively on the convoy's flank.
These were American fighting ships, manned by lads
like himself, and eager for a scrap.

The thrilling sight made Butch forget his misery
momentarily, and unconsciously he squared his
shoulders. Then suddenly overwhelmed by a recollec-
tion of his fool display of the previous morning, he
buried his face in his hands with a groan.

By the time he had regained his composure the ship
was stirring to life. Dodging behind a ventilator he
watched the mechanics wheel three Corsairs out into
the gray light and tune them up for the morning
patrol. A moment or two later the members of his
own Fighter Squadron Number Three, looking keen
and fit, stepped onto the flight deck, buckling their
helmet straps.

Lieutenant Towner was the first off, showing plenty
of daylight under his Corsair's belly as he roared
away. With the 2,000 horses under the hood catapult-

ing the plane through the air at close to 350 miles an hour he swung about in a wide circle and, climbing to 5,000 feet, waited for the others to join him.

One after another the remaining squadrons zoomed aloft, hovered for a brief moment over the ship, then roared away on their business. Red Towner's plane, the sunlight glistening on her wings, was still in sight when the last one took to the air.

His face pressed hard against the cold iron of the ventilator, Butch continued to stare disconsolately off into space long after they had disappeared from sight. Finally he pulled himself together with an effort and clumped down to the ready room. Though the place was deserted, and even lonesomer than the deck, he at least wouldn't have to look at the merchant ships that he had indirectly sworn to protect. Slumping into the nearest chair he wondered if he could ever have the privilege of entering flight data in this room.

Suddenly somebody shouted on deck and the iron ladders rang with the clatter of booted feet. Butch jumped to his feet and hurried to the flight deck as the carrier's personnel slipped smoothly and unhurriedly into their positions.

The signal officer, keen-eyed and alert, was the first to appear. His checkered paddles in his hand, he climbed quickly to his little platform. Only a jump behind him came the plane directors, fire crews and arresting men.

Meanwhile, on the starboard side, one of the destroyers, her sharp stem shearing through the waves like a knife, and bristling with guns, was already racing to the head of the convoy.

Butch's heart hammered against his ribs when a plane director shouted and pointed to the east. Fighter Squadron Number Three, or at least what remained of it, was limping home. There were only two planes in the flight, and their battered wings and bullet-riddled fuselages spoke of desperate battle somewhere in the skies.

Jerry Brewster was the first to come in. Easing his engine down, he hit the deck with a bang. He was much too fast, and for a breathless moment it seemed as if he was going to plunge off the ramp. Then his hook engaged the cross cable, and the bullet-sieved plane finally eased to a stop.

Pat Eagen's plane was even less maneuverable. Lop-sided from the terrific pounding to which she had been subjected, the craft kept losing altitude and side-slipping in a crazy unmanageable way. Ordinarily an expert flyer, seldom off the groove, Pat muffed his first try completely and was waved away by the tense-faced SO for another attempt. He had better luck next time, managing to land with a jangling of loose metal.

Pale and shaken, the big flyer clambered free of the battered plane in dead silence and faced the commander. "Fighter Squadron Number Three reporting, sir. Lieutenant Towner missing."

Immediately fantastic tales began circulating through the flattop. Gradually, however, the true story of the battle, raw and typically American, took shape. Sighting a flight of Aichie, Type 99, dive bombers, Fighter Squadron Number Three had promptly sailed into them, battling so ferociously that they had knocked out three and were wheeling to attack the remainder when a flock of Zeros zipped out from behind a cloudbank.

Zeros were the Corsairs' meat, and they tore into them with their guns blazing, blowing two of them out of the sky before Red Towner's plane was caught in a burst and went down in flames.

Pat and Jerry had followed him down just as soon as they had routed the Zeros, of course, but hadn't been able to find a single trace of him or his plane.

It was the old story of facing odds without a thought of personal danger. But as Butch listened to the account of the hopelessly unequal battle his shame and humiliation were accentuated. It was his fault that Red Towner had been lost. If Butch hadn't tried to show off with that bit of grandstand play, he might have been there to intercept the Nip that had blasted Towner.

Except for a bad shaking up, Pat and Jerry had emerged from their hazardous encounter intact. Refusing to line up, they sprawled in the wardroom under the Mess Officer's disapproving eye and guzzled hot coffee while they discussed their missing leader in low tones. Red Towner had been tops, in their estimation, and either of them would willingly have taken his place.

His clenched fists thrust savagely into his pockets, Butch was listening to Jerry tell of the reckless way the lieutenant had zipped into the Japanese planes when the loudspeaker crackled—"Ensign Barclay to Airplot at once."

Too deeply mired in dejection to realize that that meant him, Butch remained slumped in his chair till Pat snapped him out of it with a friendly poke. "That's you, flyer, better get going."

His blood running hot and cold in turn, he made his way up to Airplot and reported. Commander Steele broke off his restless pacing of the narrow office and said abruptly, "I've got a job for you, Barclay. I want you to check over the area of that fight and see if you can find any trace of the lieutenant. It's only a hunch, of course," he added a little lamely, "but it's worth trying."

"Yes, sir," Butch replied.

"Climb to 7,000 feet and strike north."

"Yes, sir."

"And ensign——"

"Yes, sir."

The commander eyed him hopefully. "We're all depending on you."

"Yes, sir."

"Then get going."

No fireman ever scrambled into his clothes faster than Butch Barclay. Quick as he was, however, the mechs were even speedier, getting his old Corsair out on the ramp and tuning it up before he reached the flight deck.

Sensing that they—and the whole ship, for that matter—were pulling for him, Butch climbed aboard the airplane, gave her the gun and took off. Coming about over the flattop in a wide turn at 7,000 feet, he acknowledged the waving hands with a wiggle of his wings and zipped north on his errand.

With the engine humming like a watch, and boring through space at some 420 miles an hour, he assured himself for the umpteenth time that there was no airplane like the Corsair and no place like the blue sky for a fighter. This was where he belonged, and where he would stay, he mentally vowed, from now on.

Jerked abruptly out of these reflections by the realization that he had reached the scene of the squadron's tangle with the enemy, he nosed down, put the screw in low pitch, and eagerly scanned the placid surface of the sea.

Finding and recognizing an object at that height wasn't going to be easy. In spite of the throttled engine the Corsair swept along at such disconcerting speed that everything below took on the semblance of a wrecked plane. Taking a chance on a stall he throttled the engine still further and dropped to within a few hundred feet of the surface. That was

better and he wasn't fooled again.

Back and forth he zoomed, quartering every inch of
the sea, till the conviction gradually forced itself upon
him that the commander's hunch had backfired and
that Red Towner had quite clearly found a watery
grave.  Bitterly disappointed, he clicked his transmitter, and contacting the carrier, advised that he was
coming in.

Suddenly he stiffened in his seat.  From the corner
of his eye he fancied he had caught the suggestion of
movement on the shore of a tiny jungle-covered island
to his left.  Coming about in a short circle he zoomed
over the spot again, all but putting the plane in a stall
as a flicker of light that might have been made by a
pocket mirror flashed in his eyes.

For an instant his hand hovered uncertainly over
the transmitter.  Then jerking it away he hedge-
hopped the trees till he spotted the tangled wreckage
of the Corsair directly beneath him.  And beside it,
partially protected by the jungle growth, was the
missing flyer, flat on his back and waving frantically.

How and where to land in the thick jungle were
problems that had Butch completely baffled for a
while.  Then, just as he was about to give up in despair
and reach for the transmitter again, he spotted an
opening in the trees.  It wasn't much more than a slash
in the green, and the ground below it looked dangerously rough, but since he had made up his mind to
land, there was nothing to do but take the chance.

Holding his breath, he nosed the Corsair down and down, wiggled in between the arching treetops, pulled sharply to the left to avoid a jutting branch, and hit the ground with a jar that rattled his teeth.

He was down but still going desperately fast. Fortunately, the ground wasn't nearly as rough as it had appeared from the air, and he had retained enough of his wits to realize that the jungle growth had been freshly cut, as if the place was being prepared for some kind of an emergency landing field.

As much concerned now with his take-off as with his landing, he swung the Corsair as close to the left as he dared, then brought the plane about in a sharp ground loop. The maneuver worked. The Corsair finally came to a stop in the middle of the clearing, ready for an immediate getaway.

The hazardous landing had taken more out of him than he realized. As he stepped to the ground he had to cling to the fuselage to keep from falling. Annoyed at this added, and totally unexpected, hazard he brushed his hand across his eyes in an impatient gesture and looked up to see a flotilla of invasion barges, crowded with soldiers, bearing down on the far side of the island. In a panic, he turned and pounded through the thickets in search of the lieutenant. With the Japanese in control of the place he hadn't a moment to lose.

He found Towner stretched out limply on the ground. The squadron leader greeted him with a

twisted  grin.  "Good  work,  ensign,  that's  one  landing
you  will  never  be  grounded  for . . ."

"Hurry,"  panted  Butch,  "the  place  is  full  of  Japs."

The  lieutenant's  face  tightened  and  he  waved  him
away.  "Better  scram  while  you  can."

But  Butch  had  no  intention  of  obeying  the  order.
Grasping  the  injured  man  under  the  arms,  he  propped
him  up  against  a  tree  and,  after  a  couple  of  back-
breaking  heaves,  managed  to  hoist  him  onto  his
shoulder  and  start  for  the  plane  at  a  clumsy  trot.  He
reached  it  just  as  the  first  barge  spilled  its  load  of
warriors  onto  the  beach.

Thankful  that  he  had  taken  the  precaution  to  give
himself  all  the  room  possible  for  a  quick  getaway,
Butch  tumbled  the  protesting  lieutenant  aboard  the
plane,  climbed  in  after  him  and  gave  her  the  gun.

Responding  to  his  touch  like  the  high-strung,  sensi-
tive  thing  she  was,  the  Corsair  went  roaring  and
coughing  down  the  clearing  like  a  runaway  tractor.
Then,  just  when  it  seemed  that  she  was  going  to  crash
into  the  thickets,  Butch  brought  her  nose  up  sharply.
There  was  a  sickening  suspicion  of  a  stall,  followed  by
a  splintering  crash  as  the  undercarriage  clipped  the
tops  of  the  trees;  then  they  were  in  the  clear.

The  enemy  below  had  still  to  be  reckoned  with,
however.  Fanning  out,  they  peppered  the  escaping
Corsair  with  everything  they  had,  from  machine  guns
to  automatic  rifles.  Butch  saw  the  instrument  board
melt  away  under  his  eyes.  Praying  that  the  vital  parts

might be spared, he gave the tight little ship all the gas she could take and shot upward in a wild surge of power that speedily put them out of range.

Restraining a wild impulse to let out a whoop, Butch contented himself with thumbing his nose at the angry soldiers below, pointed the plane south, and streaked for home. All that remained now was to find the old carrier and come in.

But his joy was short-lived. Apparently, he had merely jumped from the frying pan into the fire. Billowing up toward him came a thick blanket of fog that clouded the windshield and blotted the sea from sight. He was really in a tight spot now. With his gas reserves badly depleted, and his radio shattered, he was as helpless as a blind man. He figured that his best bet was to keep on a southerly course, no matter what happened, and was about to make a little compensation for the wind drift when the engine spluttered, coughed ominously, and went dead.

He could have hit the silk, of course, he had plenty of altitude for that—but because of his passenger he didn't give that way of escape a second thought.

Then, abruptly, through a rift in the fog, he caught sight of the carrier, dead ahead. The SO was at his post, to port of the ramp, his white flag flying and his checkered paddles obviously itching to move. Nosing the Corsair down, Butch put her in over the groove and landed on the deck with all the grace of a frozen goose with wooden legs. There was a scream of tortured metal, a spine-twisting lurch, and the plane finally ground to a smoky stop.

There was a concerted rush across the deck, but the AO was the first to reach the plane. "Glad to see you back, lieutenant," he beamed, giving Red Towner's hand a squeeze. "And good work, Barclay," he added, thumping Butch enthusiastically on the back. "I had a hunch you would make it."

The lieutenant gave a shaky laugh. "If you think this was a tricky landing you should have seen the one he made back there on the island—right into the Japs' laps."

The AO chuckled. "I can just imagine it," he said. "That's the kind of 'smart' flying I *like* to see, Barclay. Know what I mean?"

Butch grinned happily. "Yes, sir!" he replied.

# THE COWARD
## by General Edwin H. Randle

The jeep picked up speed and disappeared around a bend, leaving the lieutenant standing in the narrow dusty road. His distraught eyes contemplated a small, blue, canvas marker. It sagged between two rods thrust into the bank beside the road and bore a device he recognized. The marker told him the command post of his regiment was in the woods.

The lieutenant's slender body accepted the warm spring sunshine of northern Tunisia, but he gave it no thought. It was different from the recent winter's miserable cold and rain, nothing more. The other attributes of spring, the soft air, the birds, and the new green leaves gave him no pleasure. He did not even notice them. The lieutenant was very young, but his helmet hid that, as well as the anxiety and humiliation in his eyes.

He lingered, dreading to enter the woods, encircled by an island of peaceful, unscarred countryside. Except for a tangle of telephone lines in the ditch, and strung from tree to tree, there was no evidence of war. Not for months had he been so completely alone. He wanted to remain, but the sound of an approaching truck spoiled his feeling of isolation. With a glance at his dirty, spotted, fieldjacket and OD trousers, he walked toward a trail leading into the woods.

There was no underbrush and the tall pines, bare of branches except near the top, cast long shadows on the brown, needle-covered earth. After a time he came upon a group of small, black, rectangular tents. A sign on one read ADJUTANT, and he shambled toward it. As he drew near, a captain came out; he was bare-headed and had friendly blue eyes.

"Hello," the captain said. "Are you Carroll?"

"Yes, sir. The colonel wishes to see me?" The lieutenant hoped for a negative answer, but knew that was impossible. They'd sent for him, hadn't they?

"Yeah, but he's busy now. Wait over there with Lieutenant Osborne." The adjutant made a motion with his head. "The colonel will see you together." He turned, walked around the blackout curtain and reentered the tent.

Lieutenant Carroll was glad the colonel was busy. It was quiet here. He wished they would keep him, give him a job on the staff. But there wasn't a chance, he thought, not with his record.

Osborne was lying on his back under a tree. He was long, slim, and older than Carroll. He did not move when Carroll let the Tommy gun slip from his shoulder, leaned it against the tree trunk, and slumped to the ground.

Opposite them a wide path ran back thirty yards to a small, black wall-tent. A fly had been pitched in front. Beside the tent, on the back seat of a command car, two men were talking. Carroll recognized the colonel and lowered his eyes.

"What's he got on you?" Osborne asked, rolling over and raising himself on one elbow.

"I put in for a transfer."

"Transfer where?"

"I don't care." Nervously Carroll dug at a stone with his finger. "I'm no good at this stuff. I can't command a platoon. Those fast-shooting German machine guns paralyze me, even when they're not coming close."

"Yeah?"

"The men look at me, wanting me to tell them what to do, and I can't." He took off his helmet and dropped it beside him. His hands were shaking. "I've asked for a transfer to some rear-area job. I'm a college gradu- ate. There's lots of things I can do to help the war effort."

"Sure. Sure." Osborne agreed. He grinned and

sat up, wrapping both arms about his knees. "I'm going back, too."

"You've asked for a transfer?"

"Absolutely. I can't take it either. I've put in six years, starting as a private. Thought I was fair shakes as a soldier till El Guettar. Boy! No more of that for me! My company commander got it right through the head first day. Lots of other guys, too. You know how it was."

Yes, Carroll knew how it was, but a sudden dislike for Osborne came over him. He could not explain it, except the guy had been a soldier for six years and now wanted out of the first tough spot he'd ever been in. A quitter. With himself it was different. Some men are just not suited for combat—their nervous systems, or something. He was one of those. But he hated the way the men looked at him.

Osborne's helmet lay on the ground. He tossed a pebble at it. "Those Germans sure take good cover. From nowhere their fast-shootin' machine guns pin you down. Why don't we have machine guns that shoot that fast?"

Carroll did not answer. His eyes wandered up the trail to the colonel's tent. He closed them, hoping the fear and shame would go away. They did not.

"I didn't think we'd get into the war," he finally said. "Never really gave it much thought, I guess. Just liked the idea of being an officer."

"Well, think about it now," Osborne advised.

"How do you mean?"

"I mean, think what's goin' to happen."

"What?" Carroll looked puzzled.

"A week ago we left El Guettar and moved up here, behind the British. What's next?"

"How should I know?"

"I'll tell you. We'll relieve the Limeys, or pass through 'em. Then it'll be more of the same, machine guns, and more artillery than we've been up against yet, and we're just startin'. After Africa there's Europe. Boy, we're smart, gettin' back to the rear area."

It was growing dark. The adjutant came out of his tent and walked toward them. Behind the tents, deeper in the woods, they could hear some metal mess kits banging. Headquarters Company was finishing chow.

"The colonel will see you," the adjutant announced.

Carroll and Osborne got up, put on their helmets, picked up their Tommy guns and followed him.

The colonel sat behind a table under the fly. On the table were piles of papers, weighted down with rocks to keep them from blowing away.

"Lieutenants Carroll and Osborne, sir," the adjutant said, then started to leave. The colonel stopped him and pulled two papers from one pile, replacing the rock paperweight. In the dark they could not clearly see his face, but they had seen it before. They knew the tough, determined expression.

"I have your letters," the colonel began. His tone was conversational and Carroll's fear of him subsided a little. He and Osborne remained silent, standing at attention.

The colonel got to his feet, almost overturning the folding chair. "Now let me tell you something," he said. "No officer in this regiment is going back to a soft, safe job, while others are risking their lives every fifteen minutes, and quite a few losing them—not as long as I'm around."

He stepped back from the table, placed the metal chair in front of him and rested both hands on its back.

"Both of you accepted commissions in the infantry. You knew the implications, or should have. But now you want to crawl out of having to fight and still keep your commissions." He released the chair and folded his arms. "You can't do it."

"But, sir," Osborne broke in.

"Wait! I'm not finished." The colonel pulled at his belt. "There are two things you can do. I'll give you a choice. Number one. You can sit here and write out resignations of your commissions. I'll forward them with my approval."

He looked from one to the other. They did not speak.

"Want to hear number two?" The voice was now a little bit milder, less aggressive.

"Yes, sir," they mumbled.

"It's this. Go back and fight. *Someone* thought you'd make good officers. I'll transfer you to other battalions, but if you fail again, the other choice is still open."

"But sir, I can't lead a platoon," Carroll pleaded. "I just freeze up under fire."

"You're an ROTC graduate, aren't you? Been to Benning, haven't you?"

"Yes, sir."

"Just as soon as you decide you'd rather die than have your men know you for a yellow-livered coward, you'll be able to lead them. What's your choice?"

"I'll try, sir, if I have to."

"You don't have to. You can resign, but I won't send you to the rear."

"I'll try again."

"And you'll do all right if somewhere in you there's a teaspoonful of guts and a nickel's worth of pride. How about you, Osborne?"

"I'll go back, sir. Maybe I can do better."

They saluted and walked down the path in silence.

Osborne's prediction about the future employment of the regiment proved accurate. In a few days it relieved a British brigade at the south end of a valley. For a week it held its positions and patrolled the valley, waiting. The Germans at the north end patrolled, too, and sometimes the patrols met, but not often. Then one night the 1st Battalion was sent to seize the southernmost hill of a chain forming the valley's east boundary. The Germans had neglected to occupy it. In the dark the battalion established itself without firing a shot.

Lieutenant Carroll's new command was the 3d platoon of C Company. He was known only as an officer transferred in because lieutenants were needed. The night they moved onto the hill no one noticed how nervous he was. No one, that is, but the platoon sergeant. He helped Carroll get the platoon in position.

During the ensuing days Carroll kept to himself and avoided the other company officers. He spoke to the men only to make suggestions. They accepted his suggestions as orders. They wanted to like him and look up to him. After all he was their lieutenant. He looked after them, and he dug his own foxhole. They particularly liked the idea of his digging his own fox-hole. Two of his squads were sent out, at different times, on patrol missions. Carroll inspected them before they left and made helpful suggestions. He could do this because he spent nearly all his time remembering what he had learned in the ROTC course, and at Benning. It surprised him how much he could remember, now that he was not under fire.

One day, when they had been on the hill a week, the company commander sent for Carroll. He explained what he knew of the enemy, and told him that the big attack south of them had started.

"Our battalion," he said, "is to capture this chain

of hills. At zero-eight-hundred tomorrow, your platoon will capture the first one." He pointed to the next hill in the chain. "There will be an artillery concentration on its crest from zero-seven-four-five to zero-eight-hundred. The last salvo will be smoke. When our concentration starts, begin moving up the hill. Assault with the smoke salvo. You will be covered by all the heavy machine guns and 81-mm. mortars in the battalion. Clear?"

Carroll nodded. He did not trust himself to speak.

"Tonight," the captain continued, "move down to the base of this hill and dig foxholes from which to attack in the morning, but keep your sentinels awake. I don't want your attack spoiled by a German raid before you get started. I'll be here. . . . Any questions?"

Lieutenant Carroll could not speak. The horrible sinking feeling was back in his stomach. He nodded that he understood, and returned to his platoon.

It was mid-afternoon. The platoon sergeant looked at him expectantly, but Carroll threw himself face down in his foxhole. He closed his eyes. Except for the captain's order his mind was blank. He remembered every detail of the order, but nothing else came to him—no plans, no ideas, no promptings of things to be done. Three words began repeating themselves in in his mind, endlessly—the colonel's words, *yellow-livered coward*.

To get away from the hammering words he sat up and gazed across the valley. It was a lovely valley. On the far green hills patches of wild crimson poppies grew, great masses of them, like huge red blankets laid out in the sun on a grassy slope. There were other patches of color, too, masses of some blue flower whose name he did not know. The floral blankets of red and blue did not mingle or blend into the green of the hillsides. Their edges were sharp and distinct. Never had he seen such a brilliantly colorful natural land-scape. And on the crest of the highest hill, gleaming in the sunlight like a jewel in a crown, stood a tiny, white domed mosque, a shrine perhaps.

The lovely view and the thought of the mosque quieted his stomach and lessened the fear a little. An occasional shell whooshed overhead, but they were friendly shells and did not bother him.

The platoon sergeant had been watching. He left his foxhole and came and sat on the ground beside Carroll. A big, good-natured, second-generation Pole from Buffalo, he apparently had no nerves at all, but he had great pride. He was proud of being an American, proud of the platoon, and proud that the men thought him very brave. The fact that they thought him brave made him braver still.

"Captain have any orders?" Sergeant Zalinski asked.

Lieutenant Carroll was sitting on the edge of his foxhole, feet inside on his raincoat.

"Yes," he answered, and in a monotone repeated the order, never lifting his eyes from the raincoat.

"Not so tough," the sergeant said, when Carroll had

finished. "Not many Germans on that hill; maybe a few, maybe none."

"But they'll have flanking fire on the slopes, and mortar fire from behind the hill."

"Could be."

The sergeant gazed across the valley. His face took on an expression of embarrassment, like a boy wanting to say something nice.

After a long pause he shifted his position and said, "The platoon thinks we got a good lieutenant this time."

Carroll was startled. He raised his eyes and let them rest on the stony slope a few yards from him.

"Why should they think that," he asked.

"Well, you've looked after them, shown interest . . . and the way you instructed the patrols. . . . Your ideas worked out, especially about scouts farther out, and moving by bounds. And you dug your own foxhole; the men liked that."

"The patrol stuff is all in the book."

"Sure, but remembering it at the right time is something else."

"Wasn't my predecessor all right?" He had not meant to ask that; it slipped out.

"Him?" The sergeant laughed. "Naw. Scared to death all the time."

"What happened to him?"

"Wounded, if you want to call it that. Cut his hand on a C-ration can divin' into his foxhole. He'll get a

Purple Heart, too. German shell made him jump, and that's an act of the enemy, ain't it?"

"Who led the platoon?"

"I did. He left everything to me. To tell you the truth, Lieutenant, he was always so scared he couldn't move. The platoon carried him along, if you get what I mean, instead of the other way 'round. Nice enough guy, but no good to us."

"Don't you ever get scared, Sergeant?"

"Sure. Every time. But I keep tellin' myself, the square-heads can't hit me. Besides, I gotta take care of the platoon. We been together since Bragg."

Carroll remained silent. He gazed off across the valley, feeling weak, wishing he could keep on sitting there, but knowing he must move soon, and dreading it.

Zalinski broke the silence. "You goin' down and pick the position for tonight, or shall I?"

Carroll stood up. "Come on, we'll both go."

He was astonished at himself. It was as though someone else had made the decision, was using his body. The reaction of a cornered coward, he thought. Zalinski had been putting him on a spot, saying he was going to make the platoon a good lieutenant, rubbing it in about his predecessor. But his mind was working. "Bring a man from each squad as guide," he ordered.

The next morning at zero-seven-four-five the sun had already been up a long time, but its rays had yet to clear the steep, almost round hill that was the 3d platoon's objective. Shells came rushing at its crest, blasting up cones of rock and dirt and dust, shattering the silence with crashing, overlapping explosions. Carroll shivered in his foxhole. He had slept little; his mind, concentrated on the attack, had repelled sleep. Fear was his companion, eroding will, reducing muscles to jelly. With the shelling there came a cold, slimy emptiness in his stomach.

"Lieutenant!" Zalinski shouted from his foxhole five yards away. "Give the signal! We gotta get up there before our concentration lifts."

Carroll heard but did not move. His hands were shaking and he was sweating under the arms in spite of the morning chill. Then the sergeant was squatting beside the foxhole, looking down at him.

"What's the matter, Lieutenant?" He had to shout to penetrate the racket, and Carroll's dazed condition.

Carroll's mouth was dry. "I'm sick, Sergeant. I can't move."

The sergeant looked at him, then away. "You don't have to go," he said. "I guess you better not. It might be better. I can take the platoon, I've done it before."

"I know. I want to go, but I'm sick. I can't move."

"Yeah. I know how it is." Zalinski was sympathetic. "Why not try to join us when we've taken the hill. Maybe you'll feel better then."

The big man sprang up. Carroll heard him shout, "Come on, you guys!" Then he heard nothing but shells exploding five hundred yards away on the next crest. His mouth felt like cotton and he reached for his canteen. Trembling hands made it hard to unscrew the cap. When he tried to drink, some of the water ran down his chin. Now they'd send him home in disgrace, after he'd resigned his commission.

He thought of Zalinski and the platoon—what was left of it after El Guettar. He liked them. They thought he was going to make them a good platoon leader—or did Zalinski make that up. If he waited until the concentration lifted and they had the hill, and he wasn't with them, they would look at him as the men had in his other platoon. He dreaded their contempt; he was an officer, supposed to set an example. Maybe the colonel was right. Maybe it was better to die than disappoint those men he liked, see their respect turn to contempt. Maybe death wasn't so bad if it came quickly. Better that than hate himself the rest of his life.

The hand that reached for his Tommy gun was trembling. He rose to a stooping position and staggered out of the foxhole. His legs were numb, but they supported him and gravity took him the few yards into the gully between hills. He expected to hear fast-shooting machine guns, but booming artillery behind and crashing shells on the hill ahead overpowered every other sound.

"They can't hit me," he muttered as he started up the hill. His legs wanted to give way but he made them push. Soon he was gasping for breath. The slope was

steep and rocky. Loose stones made his feet slip and held him back. Last chance, he thought. Catch up before the concentration lifts, or go home a yellow-livered coward.

He was gaining, clawing his way, making his legs shove harder. They felt stronger and he was no longer trembling. Behind him a fearful clatter erupted. The heavy machine guns, eight of them, were pouring out lead in conical streams. He glanced at his watch. He still had three minutes. He must make it, must catch up. Now he was crawling on hands and knees. His stomach did not bother him, he felt better. Mixed with the roar of the machine guns were the hollow belchings of the 81s. Machine guns were boxing in the platoon, covering its flanks, the mortars shelling the reverse slope, searching it.

The platoon, Carroll saw, was crawling now, nearing the concentration. Zalinski crawled and waved his arm, urging on some who were a little behind. Carroll scrambled toward him; it was only a few yards. He ducked his head, crouching double, gasping for breath. The racket was terrific, but he was glad, it meant the concentration was still falling and he was in time. Somehow the crashing din was exhilarating. He felt excited. His helmet slipped forward obstructing his vision. He pushed it back. With one wild leap he threw himself beside the sergeant.

Zalinski turned his head. His eyes opened wide. He said something. Carroll grinned. The sergeant pointed ahead. A dense white cloud was forming on the crest. As it billowed a breeze began drifting it slowly off the crest and on toward the next hill beyond.

"Let's go," Carroll yelled. He scrambled to his feet and ran. They must get to the crest before the smoke completely dispersed.

The machine guns and mortars were still firing, though the artillery had stopped. Zalinski was right behind. They ran through the prone platoon, shouting and waving their arms. The men got up and followed. Then the wind changed. Slowly the smoke cloud drifted back until once again it precisely enveloped the crest before them. The machine guns and mortars ceased firing. Carroll stopped at the edge of the smoke. The platoon stopped too.

"Far enough," he called. "The enemy can shell the crest, too." No longer did he have to yell. The only sound was a ringing in his ears. Not a shot anywhere. Sheep were peacefully grazing in the lovely valley below. The men of the platoon were watching him expectantly, their eyes friendly, respectful.

"Flank squads enfilade the reverse slope," he ordered. "Center squad dig here. Sergeant Zalinski, check the casualties."

The flank squads moved off. Men of the center squad slipped off their packs and spread out. Carroll relaxed. The muscles of his legs were trembling, but he felt good—and proud. Unfastening his entrenching shovel he started digging behind the center squad.

Sergeant Zalinski came up. "I'll do that, Lieutenant, if you want to check the flank squads," he offered. "And there ain't no casualties."

Carroll straightened up. "What! What did you say?"

Zalinski grinned. "I said there ain't no casualties."

"No casualties!" The questioning expression was replaced by a slow grin. He threw down his shovel. "Sergeant, there wasn't a German on this hill, was there?"

The sergeant guffawed. "I been watchin' this hill for a week. Was almost positive it wasn't occupied." He shucked off his combat pack, laid it on the ground, and glanced up at Carroll. "We sure had us one swell fight, anyway, didn't we?"

Carroll unfastened the chinstrap and pulled off his helmet. He looked sheepish, yet proud. "I had a good fight," he said.

The sergeant smiled.

Encouraged, Carroll said, "Tomorrow, Sergeant, we'll have to take a hill with Germans on it. But I think I'll be just ordinary scared—not paralyzed."

"Yes, sir, Lieutenant, that's right," Zalinski replied. "And like I said, the platoon thinks we got us a pretty good lieutenant this time."

# BLITZKRIEG
## by John R. Tunis

"One thing for sure, in this mess no French traffic cop is going to stop us for our licenses," said Marvin.

The British boy at the wheel was blond, with a long nose under the cap he had pulled down over his eyes. He nodded.

"Right!" That was all he said. There was a grimness in his tone. It matched the scene around them.

Far ahead on *Route Nationale 10,* the main highway which stretched directly south from Paris to the Spanish border, the boys in the little car could see a chaos of autos, buses, trucks, army vehicles, farm carts, horse-drawn old carriages heavy with dust—all packed bumper-to-bumper down the long, straight poplar-lined highway. The only order in that scene of disaster was a small column of English people of which the two boys were a part.

Time: June, 1940. Place: France. The entire northern part of the country had suddenly been over-run by the German Army. General Guderian's Panzers were cutting across France to the coast, then turning and slicing toward Paris, the capital and heart of the nation. It was as if the United States had been invaded by a foreign army from the north, an army occupying everything from Boston to Chicago, ready-ing itself for a leap to seize New York and Washington.

One morning there was spring, peace, sunshine, fruit trees in bloom. The next day, planes roaring overhead, tanks, artillery and motorized infantry breaking through the front lines, surprising French troops in the rear, tearing northwestern France from the rest of the country. This blitzkrieg, the lightning war, the war that never struck twice in the same place, was here in one town, then there, then twenty miles away, sowing defeat and disaster everywhere it hit. This was the stroke that stuns an army by its unexpect-edness, that spreads panic, blows up ammunition dumps, machine-guns convoys of reserves rushing to the front, that fights not merely soldiers but the entire civilian population.

Like so many others that sunny June morning, those two fifteen-year-old boys in that battered Austin were fleeing Paris. Marvin Reynolds, son of the chief of an American broadcasting company in Europe, had his *permis de conduire,* or driver's license. Christopher Norton, his friend at school, whose father was an Englishman and correspondent for a London newspaper, had neglected to get his although he was a good driver.

Their families were close friends, the boys in the same class at school. When the British Embassy decided to send a caravan of twenty cars with women and children south to safety in Bordeaux, from where they could be evacuated to England by boat, it was decided that the boys should leave also. Chris was to go along with the embassy crowd by boat at Bordeaux; Marvin was to wait two days for his parents to meet him at the Hotel Majestic. His mother had written the two words "Hotel Majestic" on five sheets of notepaper, put one in each of three of his pockets, and two others in his suitcase.

They were glad to leave. Fear covered Paris that morning. The newspapers were down to four pages, shops and stores were closing as owners left to escape the oncoming Germans. Nobody wanted to be in the city when the Nazis arrived. Early that morning, Marvin, leaning over the balcony of their fifth-story apartment, had observed *gendarmes,* local police, patrolling the streets two-by-two on bicycles. Marvin had also noticed that each man had a rifle slung over his shoulder, and they were spotchecking passersby. He called this information to his father who was at the breakfast table reading the French morning paper.

"H'm. Things must be really bad if they're doing that."

Then Marvin heard a low rumble in the distance. It was a kind of continuous low thunder, ominous and frightening. "What's that noise?"

His father listened carefully. "German artillery. They're firing at the disordered French. Where? Not far; out on the River Marne, probably. It won't be long now. You boys are getting out just in time."

So Chris and Marvin—well-briefed, and with food, maps and money—were excited that morning as they drew up at the British Embassy. It was a part of history, and they were living it; they knew this, felt it. Some day they would be talking about it, telling folks how they escaped from Paris during the invasion with the German Army so close you could hear their guns on the Marne.

Just before eight, the caravan in a long line pushed out of the cobblestoned courtyard of the embassy on the *Rue St. Honoré,* escorted by two trim British officers in khaki, each seated in a motorcycle sidecar with an enlisted man driving. The officer had a pistol strapped to his belt, and Marvin noticed that there were five cans of gasoline strapped on the back of each sidecar. He approved his father's foresight in scrounging six or seven cans for their own car, now safely locked in the trunk in back. Gas was not only rationed; with the Germans approaching the city it was pure gold. All gas stations were sold out.

Now they moved rapidly through empty, silent streets. Major Grant, the assistant military attaché in charge of the convoy, was moving up and down the line in his sidecar. A megaphone was strapped to his chest.

"Keep together, please, close up there . . . keep together."

The road was straight and clear through deserted suburbs, until finally they reached that endless traffic jam on the main highway, Route 10, the road south. A French traffic policeman saluted Major Grant, looked at his papers, passed the British column through.

On the road ahead was a mixture of people and vehicles that kept the pace down to a walk. What seemed like the entire population of Holland, Belgium and northern France jammed that road. Added to them were the cars with strange license plates the boys had never seen before, many of the cars overheated from constant stop-and-go driving, radiators steaming. All of the vehicles were packed with kids, cats, dogs, parrots and birds in cages, and some automobiles had mattresses tied on top for protection.

The two boys looked at each other quickly. Each had the same thought as they started, moved slowly for ten yards, stopped and moved again.

"Maybe this isn't going to be fun after all."

The boys fell silent. The high excitement of early morning had vanished. The sun rose higher and hotter. They had been driving several hours under horrible conditions. Their heads ached from the fumes of escaping gasoline, their throats were parched, they were hungry, hot, tired. Their faces were streaked with the dust from a hundred automobiles up ahead. No, decidedly, this was not adventure. This was war. War was not fun.

About noon they reached the bridge across the river Loire at the city of Tours. To get south, everyone had to pass over that bridge and traverse the city. Three main roads converged at the entrance to the bridge; consequently there was a wait of half an hour while the French traffic brigade on duty was handling the mob waiting to get across. At the orders of the major, the British group brought out some food.

The two boys were hungry; they gobbled the food prepared by their parents, and drank Coca-Cola. Meanwhile, around them in the village, from its stables and sheds, every kind of wheeled contrivance was edging into the narrow streets. There were new Peugeots, old Citroëns, ancient farm carts that for half a century had lain untouched under layers of dust. Even the village fire engine was being cranked up. Beside each vehicle stood men and women holding bulging bedsheets. Marvin jumped out, a sandwich in his mouth, to watch, then turned away, ashamed. Each sheet was full of treasures wrenched from fireside, wall or table. Panic had seized the village. After watching that flood of refugees roll past day and night for almost a week, they had fallen victims, too.

The major passed by, wiping sweat from the inside of his khaki cap with a red silk handkerchief. A woman rushed from an alley, and seeing an officer, grabbed his arm.

*"M'sieur,* the major, please come here."

Chris and Marvin, who stood beside their small Austin, watched the major turn.

"Where? What's the matter?" he asked.

"We're evacuating. We're leaving. Come," she urged, pulling his arm.

The face of the major became stern. "In God's name, why? Look at this mess on the road! The whole of France is doing the same thing right now. We're foreigners here, we have to leave the country or we'll end up in a prison camp. But you won't. You're in your own land. Don't you see, Madame, you'd be far better off at home than in this . . . chaos . . . this mess . . ." He used the word *déroute,* and Marvin, who spoke the language, observed that his French was excellent. "Tell me, why are you leaving?"

"Nobody knows, quite. Orders of the mayor. Please *M'sieur* the major, be kind enough to give us a hand, please."

"Of course. But what is it you want? We have no room in our party."

"No, no, it's our car. My husband is an officer at the front. He left the car. I've had the tires filled up, the battery in, and I have some gasoline, but I don't know

how to start it. I have never driven a car, but I know
I can if it is started. The traffic moves so slowly. It
would be easy."

Easy to drive? On that highway where they made
10 or 15 miles an hour, stopping every few hundred
yards, shifting gears, changing from low to second,
then to top, then back again, and again, and again.

"My dear Madame, you would break down before
you got to the end of that city over there. Impossible.
Sorry. There would be constant shifting of gears, over-
heating, and other problems. You could not possibly
do it. You must excuse me." He gave her a quick,
British salute, and passed along the column.

The woman stood for a moment, looking after him
and cursing. Marvin had never seen a respectable
woman so upset. It troubled him as he turned back to
his car.

Finally the convoy passed over the bridge and got
through the city. When they were out on the main
road once more, the major came alongside their car.
Soon the convoy would take a side road to the right,
longer but traffic-free. He indicated on a map the
towns through which they would pass: Parthenay,
Niort, Saintes. Then he showed how they would come
back to Route 10 just above the city of Bordeaux, their
destination.

"Hold on to that map, lad. Someone will steal it if he
can. Maps are gold right now. There isn't a map to be
bought in all Paris, and none around here, so watch it."

"Yes, sir," said Marvin, who was at the wheel. He thrust the map deep into his pocket. He faced the real test of a driver. The cars around them were roaring, steaming, smoking, dropping out frequently. At times they passed a car hauled to the side of the road, occasionally with a shattered windshield and bullet holes in it. In one such automobile three passengers lay lifeless; blood seeped from the closed doors. The procession was too busy with their own troubles to bother.

So it went, everyone for himself, each driver snatching an advantage, edging ahead, breaking every rule of the road. Behind each wheel was a weary man or woman; one car full of grownups had a boy of twelve at the wheel. Many of these people had been on the road from the north five days and nights without sleep.

At a crossroads before a town, the procession was held up by a column of tanks moving counter to the main road. As they waited, Marvin noticed a boy, perhaps eleven or twelve, standing nearby. He was wearing shorts, and by the hand he held a slip of a girl, who was crying in great sobs.

The boy's eyes were searching the long file desperately. He came toward the Austin.

"Please, sir, food! Food for my little sister. She hasn't eaten since yesterday."

Marvin looked at them. "Where are you two kids going?"

"To Bordeaux, sir, to my grandfather's. Our parents

were both killed in an air raid at Vendôme last night. Please, sir, food for my little sister, anything at all. She hasn't eaten since last night."

The little girl's sobs grew louder. The two boys in the car glanced at each other as the file of tanks, pennants flying, rumbled across the road before them.

The words of their parents were in their ears.

Promise, boys. You promise. Promise you won't pick up anyone along the road. Promise now, you won't. Especially girls. That's a promise? You promise? I promise, Dad. Yes, Mother, we won't pick anybody up.

Marvin looked at Chris, then at the weeping child beside the car. Already the rear tank had roared across their path, the column was starting to move, and a sharp warning HONK from the car behind jarred him. As if ten yards meant anything in that mess! Marvin was irritated. He leaned from the window and shouted back:

*"Fiche-moi-le-paix."* His French was full of slang phrases picked up at school. "Go soak your head." Then he beckoned to the two despairing youngsters beside the road, without thought of his solemn promises, without asking Chris.

"C'mon, Buddy, jump in."

He surprised himself. He was, as his mother liked to tell her friends, "reliable." Ask Marvin to do something, he does it. Whereas Chris, well, Chris was different. Once he had been seen walking down the

Champs Élysées with A Girl. True, the girl turned out to be only fifteen; but she was, obviously, A Girl. Yet now it was Marvin, the reliable one, the elder by six months, who had broken down, disobeyed his parents and asked those two youngsters into the overloaded car. The impulse was stronger than his promise, his training, his obligation to his parents. He found it impossible to leave those two children beside that insane cavalcade any longer.

The French boy seemed motionless with surprise for an instant. For hours cars of all kinds—large and small, old and new—driven by their countrymen and women had moved past. Nobody had stopped for them or given them a sandwich, or even a kind word.

So they had almost given up hope as hour after hour cars went by without stopping. Then this invitation from strangers! The boy sprang to action, yanked open the back door and pushed his sister inside. The rear seat was piled high with suitcases containing clothes belonging to the boys' parents, so the two youngsters squeezed into cramped positions on the floor.

The little girl was still sobbing.

Marvin's voice was cracked and dry. "I don't hardly b'lieve Dad would call her a girl, d'you, Chris? Break open some of those sandwiches, she's hungry."

Half a dozen questions from Marvin brought out a few facts. Their name was Dupont, which is like Smith in France. Lucien was thirteen, Germaine, his sister, eight. They lived in the city of Lille in the north, where their father was an official of a cotton mill. When the Germans got closer and closer and began bombing the city, he packed his family into their Citroën and started south. They skirted around Paris, and outside the town of Vendôme both parents were killed in an air raid by low-flying Heinkels of the *Luftwaffe,* the German flying corps. Had they all stayed in the car and not rushed for safety beside the road under the trees, they might . . .

At this recital the little girl again burst into uncontrollable sobs. Her brother tightened his grip and held her tight on the floor of the car, kissing and trying to soothe her. Turning in the front seat, Marvin realized how much this boy of thirteen had endured since the death of his parents the day before. It showed in his face. He was, Marvin thought, older than most American boys of twenty.

The side road they were moving along was almost empty. Gas being rationed and hard to get, few cars were used unless necessary, and once off the main highway they had the road to themselves. The British convoy began to make time, moving along at 20, then 30, then 40 to 50 miles an hour. It seemed like 100 after the pace of the morning.

In a whirl of dust and honking horns they passed through numerous towns: Pouzages, Richebonne, Fontenay-le-Comte. Then they raced up a hill and were on top of a gentle slope leading gradually to a town below, when Chris spoke.

"Blast!"

Marvin instantly knew by the jogging motion of the car what had happened. Chris pulled out to the side of the road.

Ahead, in a vast cloud of dust and haze, the column steamed on, leaving them in the hot sun beside the road. But the keen-eyed major spotted them, and raced back in his sidecar.

"What seems to be the trouble, boys?"

"We have a flat tire, sir."

"Have you got another one?"

"Yes, sir, in the rear."

"Do you know how to change it? Got all the tools? Need any help?"

"No, sir, we can change it all right. But it will take some time 'cause the spare is packed in the back with baggage."

"Very good. If you boys have things under control, I'll let you handle it. Where's your map? There . . . we go on . . . here . . . through Parthenay, that's about eighteen kilometers, then straight on to Niort, that's forty more, due south on 138. At Niort we stop half an hour for tea; you ought to catch us there easily. However, we shall leave a contact to wait your arrival. That quite clear?"

They agreed, and he tore off again in pursuit of the column vanishing in the distance. It was a reassuring thought that in the midst of all that empty loneliness,

somewhere in a fixed place someone would be watching
for them. Yet both boys suddenly felt alone and
deserted on that hilltop.

Just as they were finishing changing the tire an
ancient farm cart, creaking and groaning, suddenly
appeared over the rise behind. Two weary, panting
horses were pulling the cart. The man at the reins
was a soldier in horizon blue; another French soldier
was on each side. They were obviously fleeing like
everyone else. The cart came toward them and
stopped. One soldier jumped down from the high seat.
He had not shaved for a week. His uniform was torn,
dusty, stained. Evidently he had been in battle. His
face was cold and hard. There was no friendliness in
him.

"À qui cette voiture?" he asked hoarsely. "Whose
car?"

A second man leaped from the farm cart, an automatic pistol in one hand. He stuck the gun abruptly
into Marvin's ribs and motioned the boys backward.

"Sauvez-vous," he said curtly. "Get lost!"

Chris angrily took one step forward when the third
man, a tall, dark-haired ruffian, jumped down with a
rifle in his hand. Deserters, thought Marvin. Men like
that would not hesitate to use their guns in this spot.
Neither boy had ever looked at a rifle from that end
before.

Then the first man stepped into the driver's seat,
kicked the starter, and the others immediately piled

after him. The front springs sagged under the weight
of the three adults. With a terrific roar of the engine,
a wrenching jerk forward, the car moved. Then came
another jerk, a noise of grinding gears and it tore
away.

Beside them on the road, the two farm horses stood
shaking their heads, panting. Angrily Lucien dropped
the hand of his sister. He stood there, legs apart, looking after his retreating countrymen, furious with rage.

*"Ah, les voyous . . . les voyous . . ."* he shouted.

"The cads!" It was the only term he could think of
to express his contempt for his countrymen, as the
car of his friends disappeared in its own dust cloud.

The village was small. The cobbled main street
wound through the town, houses on each side with
window boxes red with geraniums. Everywhere there
were signs of flight and disorder as the farm cart driven
by Marvin—who had never driven a team of horses
before—came slowly down the main street. The few
stores on both sides had their shutters up; on most was
a pathetic sign written in ink: *Closed on Account of
the Mobilization.* Which meant the owner was away
with the army.

They stopped before a café, the only place showing
any signs of life, and the two boys entered. A tiny bell
jangled as they did so.

The owner, a large woman in dingy black, was seated
at a high desk to one side, watching a slovenly servant
wash the floor. Nobody spoke, nobody greeted them,

neither woman responded to their entrance in any way. Chris, whose French was excellent, spoke up.

*"Bon jour, Mesdames,"* he said. The woman at the desk grunted, no more. She looked up as the two French youngsters, still hand-in-hand, entered, and the bell tinkled again. Then Chris began to tell their story. He was eloquent as he described their flat tire, then the theft of the car by the French soldiers with guns. Gone, he said, gone, their car and all their baggage, all their clothes. The woman listened, became interested. Then indignant.

"Ah . . . *alors* . . . deserters, most likely." Her sympathy was now aroused. Chris explained they had somehow to reach Bordeaux, where Marvin's parents were due in two days.

The fat lady behind the desk rose. She was enormous.

"Gaby," she shrieked suddenly at the servant. "Gaby!" The servant looked up from the floor. "Gaby, find the Docteur Bossuet, see whether he has left yet. He was to go to Bordeaux this very afternoon to fetch his old mother, perhaps he will take you two boys along also."

At this the little girl, fearful at being left behind with her brother, began to sob loudly. "And the children also?" asked Marvin. He felt he could not desert them now.

"Ah, yes," said the woman. As the servant, wiping her hands on her apron, went out the door, the little bell tinkled. "Ah, yes, if he has room in his car, the children also."

The fat lady came down from her stand behind the desk and began to bustle about in the rear of the room. Presently she appeared with heavy cups of hot coffee, milk for the youngsters, and hard rolls, obviously several days old. The four sat down at a table, eating eagerly. They were all hungry.

Soon the servant returned, panting. Yes, Madame, the Doctor Bossuet was there in his office, he was treating a patient, he would leave in half an hour. But he was carrying gasoline for the return trip in the trunk of his car, so there was no room for baggage.

The two boys looked at each other and laughed.

"We have no baggage. Our baggage has gone ahead!"

Before long the Doctor Bossuet appeared, a big bear of a man with a beard that covered his whole vest. He listened to the account of the theft of their car, told with indignation and many gestures by the owner of the café. He shook his head in disgust, and agreed that the men were probably deserters. Yes, there was room in his small Renault, but it would be necessary for the little girl to sit on her brother's lap.

The lady refused to take money for their food, so off they went, the doctor shaking his head that Frenchmen would steal a car from two boys. He sighed.

"Ah, well, that's war for you. That's what it does to people." It appeared he was going to Bordeaux—an

hour's drive—to take his old mother back to safety, as
the city was being bombed nightly by the Italian Air
Force.

"*Ces sacrés Macaronis,*" he said angrily. It seemed
the Italians had entered the war at the last moment on
the winning side, and were helping the Germans by
bombing roads and towns in the rear of the French
army.

The ancient Renault creaked and groaned, protested
and sighed as it struck a bump in the road, and the
boys wondered whether the springs would hold up.
But the doctor kept on, asking them questions about
the theft of their Austin as they drove toward the
setting sun.

At Niort they caught up with a British motorcyclist
who had been assigned to wait for Marvin and Chris.
The column had gone on, and seeing they were in
good hands, he roared off ahead to overtake it. Finally
they perceived a cloud of smoke on the horizon. It
grew larger as they drew nearer the main highway they
had left earlier, and Marvin realized it was dust, that
once again they were joining the Paris-Bordeaux road,
Route No. 10. A large sign beside them gave the
name of the town they were nearing.

*St. Andre dé Cubsac.*

Underneath was written; *Bordeaux, 25 kilometres.*

Then they were twenty miles away. A short distance
beyond was the main highway. When they reached it,
the doctor stopped short. He had no other choice.

The highway was one gigantic traffic jam; just as it had been all the way from Paris to Tours. Cars, trucks, motor bikes, an ambulance with wounded soldiers, a fire engine, a steam roller, anything that would move was jammed close, all fleeing from the on-coming German army. There was an aged grandmother perched on sacking across the handlebars of a bicycle, two bikes hooked together to form a kind of catamaran. The father and mother had a pole over their shoulders from which hung their possessions in a sack. A small boy sat on the saddle strapped to his father's waist, a young girl clung to her mother's back. As the boys watched, fascinated, a pretty girl on roller skates, a knapsack on her back, went by, weaving in and out of traffic and making far better progress than the motor cars.

A group of dispirited, leaderless boys of eleven or twelve slumped beside their car.

"Where are you boys going?" asked Chris. They shook their heads. They had no idea. They were homeless, hopeless, abandoned, like half the people in that long file.

Finally the doctor seized his chance, wedged into the line of traffic, and slowly, foot by foot, the procession passed through the narrow street of town. It took them almost half an hour to reach the other end. By this time they were definitely moving into the setting sun.

Several kilometers beyond the town the road passed

over a river spanned by a narrow suspension bridge. The bridge was so small that there was a bottleneck at its entrance, with traffic foaming up and cars trying ruthlessly to shove their way in. Suddenly, far in the distance was the roar of engines. Instantly every motor stopped grinding.

"Jump!" screamed the doctor. "Jump, or we shall all be murdered where we stand!"

Marvin and Chris dragged the boy and the girl to the side of the road under some high linden trees. Everyone stretched flat, covering their heads as sixty express trains came down from the heavens. Thunder crashed up and down the road when the bombs fell.

"Thrump . . . thrump . . . thrump . . ."

Marvin could hear them striking the pavement at regular intervals, and the horrible explosions that ensued. On one side of him a man leaned over on his elbow and shook his fist.

"*Ah, dirty beasts!*" he cried.

Marvin looked up also. It was a terrifying sight. A massive Italian bomber roared down upon the defenseless road. Machine-gun bullets went rat-tat-tat on the pavement, spanked the sides of cars, penetrated gas tanks, drew here and there a sudden burst of flames. Then, majestic, slowly, indifferent and under no pressure from planes or anti-aircraft fire, they zoomed high into the sky.

So this is it, thought Marvin. This is war. This is how the parents of those frightened children were killed in the north. He half rose to find he was trembling all over. It had happened so quickly there had been no time to be scared, but now he was really frightened. A man up the road groaned in agony, a child shrieked. The machines made a *virage*, or turn in the sky, and raced down on the defenseless highroad again.

Once more everyone hugged the ground. Once more, the bombs fell. The ground seemed to rise as the missiles hit the pavement with a crash.

Dusk comes late to France in June. It was nearly nine o'clock and still light when they eventually worked their way across the packed bridge and into the city of Bordeaux. There it was intended to leave the two children in care of their grandparents.

The streets were foaming with people, jammed with cars, trucks and military vehicles of every make and nationality. On the sidewalks passed the armies of the Allies: French officers from all branches of the army, Poles in blue uniforms with their square, peculiar caps, Belgians in khaki, British staff officers with red tabs on the lapels of their jackets, Dutch, Norwegians, even a few Czechs. Hundreds of soldiers, sailors and airmen mingled with the throng of refugees aimlessly moving back and forth in search of food and shelter—which were rarely to be found. Bordeaux, a city of 300,000, was trying to feed and lodge a million and a half persons from the north. At every corner there was a wait and a traffic jam, with Boy Scouts in

shorts attempting to help the occasional traffic police-
men, and allow official government cars the right of
way.

The children's grandparents, Monsieur and Madame
Bonnard, lived at Rue Lecocq. The doctor stuck his
beard from the car window several times to ask the
way, and at last they discovered a quiet side street by
that name. The girl, quivering with excitement,
anxious to see a familiar face, began calling out the
numbers of the houses they passed.

"Twelve, sixteen . . . no, it must be the opposite
side. Twenty-three . . . twenty-seven . . . thirty-one . . .
thirty-five . . ."

Suddenly, without warning, she burst into tears.
Right ahead where Number 45 should have been was
an empty space. The block of houses looked like a
mouth from which a front tooth has been pulled.

Neither Chris nor Marvin had ever seen a bombed
house before. The building was shorn off cleanly from
both sides as if cut by a knife. They got out awk-
wardly, cramped and stiff from the long ride, the little
girl still sobbing. That three- story brick building was
now a heap of rubble, beams sticking up from what
had once been the cellar. Wisps of smoke rose in the
air. Anyone in that home was underneath tons and
tons of bricks and stone.

The doctor, Chris, and Marvin stood with the two
youngsters, looking at the depressing scene. Suddenly
a woman left the small group of curious onlookers

who stood around the bombed-out site, rushed toward them, and flung her arms around the little girl. In a minute she was joined by an elderly man, their grand-father, who also swept up the children in his arms. The bombed house was Number 41, the home of the Bonnards was two doors away, shaken but unharmed.

Once he had deposited the children with their grandparents, the doctor took Chris and Marvin to his mother's house for the night. The next morning after breakfast, he left them in front of the Thomas Cook travel agency in the center of the city, where they were to meet the crowd from the British Embassy.

From Bordeaux it was a ride of an hour to a place called Le Verdon at the mouth of the river Gironde where the whole group were to be taken off by a British cruiser, the *Ad Astra*.

"Why don't you come along to London with us, Marv?" asked Chris. "Look, you'd better take this chance to get out of France while you can. Your dad will understand."

"Yes, he might," reflected Marvin. "Only he told me to meet him tomorrow at noon at the Hotel Majestic where he wired for a room."

"A room, a room!" Chris repeated with scorn. "Rooms are pure gold in this town. They wouldn't reserve a room if he had wired them a thousand dollars."

"Probably not. But he'll show just the same, and so must I."

"Send him a wire. Leave a note at the hotel desk for him. Tell him you've escaped to London. My family will take care of you. And you'd be off his hands."

"Fat chance of any telegram being delivered in this mess. Nope, I really think I shouldn't. I disobeyed him taking those kids along in the car, I better stick it out and meet him when he arrives with Mother."

"Well, come out to Le Verdon, come out where we pick up the cruiser. You can grab a ride back to town in one of those cars."

So once again Chris and Marvin set out in the long British procession. The road was flat, along a peninsula with huge vineyards on each side. After a ride of an hour they neared the end, came to a pine grove, swung past a Polish army camp where a Polish flag was being lowered. Before long they overtook a column of trucks with Polish troops in battle dress. Then all at once they were out of the pine groves and on the dunes in bright sunlight. Before them lay the sparkling water of the bay. Just ahead was a long, gray cruiser flying the British Union Jack.

Never did a warship seem so beautiful to Marvin as that taut, efficient-looking vessel with its bristling anti-aircraft guns. With all his heart he wanted to ride her to London. Surely his father would understand, would probably be happy to have him safe and sound and out of harm's way. For a few seconds he wavered. Then he put the idea away from him.

Below was a small pier, and tied to the pier was a

kind of ferryboat already loaded with Polish troops piling off trucks. The British crowd got out of their cars and quickly filed on after them. Then came more trucks with more Poles.

"I'll go out with you to the cruiser," suggested Marvin.

"Marv, look, you ought to take this chance while it's offered, you ought to come to London, you know you should. See here, you may miss your dad entirely, then what? It's possible, y'know, in a mess like Bordeaux right now. Come on, I can fix it up for you, and you have your passport. How much cash do you have?"

Marvin looked at his wallet. He had three American dollars and about a hundred francs, some twenty dollars in all. Chris watched him count his reserves. "Suppose you don't happen to connect with your father. How long will that last?"

Marvin hated to think. Before he could reply Major Grant interrupted them. "Now then, step lively boys, we haven't a lot of time, y'know. We're pulling out immediately. Step lively everyone, please, no time to waste."

"C'mon, Marvin, let's go," urged Chris.

The ferry was a small craft of several thousand tons, used for transportation of passengers and cars from Le Verdon to Royan across the water. Forward was a raised deckhouse. Several thousand Polish troops with suitcases and bundles of all kinds were packed into every inch of space amidships.

Major Grant pushed Chris aboard, looked around, waved to the French captain in the deckhouse as Marvin leaped aboard too. Instantly the gangplank was hauled back, the ferry gave a short, sharp snort, and open water appeared between vessel and pier. In a few minutes that gray warship which seemed so small from the hillside above the dunes, loomed large and secure above them. Sailors dropped down a gangplank, and immediately a British naval officer took over.

"Hurry, please hurry up," the naval officer commanded them. The British travelers picked up their bags and suitcases and edged toward the gangplank, faces aglow at the idea of being aboard a British ship.

"Last chance, Marv. Come on lad, come on. You really should come, you know. France is in a mess now. Your dad will understand. C'mon, hurry . . ."

That cruiser towering above them looked safe, powerful, reassuring. Yet he knew he shouldn't leave. His orders were to meet his father in Bordeaux; some time, somehow his father would get there. He must be waiting for him.

The British had all gone up the gangplank. "Hurry, boys, hurry up now," said Major Grant.

"Do come, please. Marv, this is your last chance."

"I know it. I'm sorry, Chris, I'd like to but I oughtn't. Go ahead, and good luck."

They shook hands. Chris turned reluctantly and

went up the gangplank, followed by the two sailors, Major Grant and the naval officer.

All at once there was a piercing noise from above. A siren sounded, a horrible wail, now high, now lower. Without warning the gangplank fell away from the deck of the cruiser just as the naval officer was hauled aboard.

Chris was leaning over the rail. "How much money did you say?"

"About twenty dollars." The gap between warship and ferry was widening.

Chris hastily emptied his purse of some cards, jammed the money deep inside, and tossed it onto the deck of the ferry. A sailor picked it up and handed it to Marvin who shoved it deep into his inside pocket.

"Thanks! Thanks lots, Chris. I won't forget. I'll need it." He had to shout with his hands around his mouth for now there was a lot of open water between them, and the cruiser was gaining speed. Marvin could see sailors running for their gun stations, and others shoving the passengers away from the rail and below.

The tug turned, its propeller churning furiously, gathered speed too, anxious to put as much space as possible between itself and the cruiser. Marvin spotted the planes, three of them, coming in from the sun. A large powerful anti-aircraft battery on the cruiser's stern went into action.

On the ferry the French crew lined the rails like spectators at a football game, watching the contest between pursued and pursuer. The cruiser was making speed now, smoke pouring from its funnels. Above, the planes bored in, twisting, dipping, taking evasive action, turning and bending to avoid the guns below. They were obviously Italians.

Then suddenly the warship vanished. Two enormous waterspouts hid her from everyone on the ferry. Marvin held his breath, expecting an explosion, but then the vessel appeared, cleaving clouds of foam, rocking violently from side to side. It appeared to be untouched. Every gun seemed to be blazing.

A deep shout came to him through the noise. He turned. A sailor was tossing his white cap in the air. Marvin looked out again and saw a plane fluttering like a bird in trouble, descending, then spinning down faster and faster, until it hit the water. There was a loud explosion.

The other planes, high in the heavens by this time, swung around and lazily vanished into the sun. In the far distance the cruiser, still gathering speed, headed straight for safety and the open sea.

Marvin turned back to where several cars were starting the journey back to Bordeaux, to ask for a ride. Suddenly he felt utterly alone.

He did not know how he was ever going to wait two endless days until his parents came. But he knew that somehow he would find the patience to do it.

# DESERT RAIDERS

## by John B. Stanley

There were ten of them.

In the moonlight of the early North African evening, as he looked at them, Keith thought of how fit they all looked. These were *real* soldiers, he told himself, and if anyone could do the job that lay ahead, these men could. A sense of pride surged through him, and he was thankful for the fate that had made him their commander. His gaze shifted from face to face. Then suddenly a twinge of anxiety shook him. He wasn't sure whether it was caused by his concern for the entire group; but he was disturbed. There flashed through his mind, in a kaleidoscopic series, the misfortunes that might befall his little band on this raid behind Rommel's line.

A moment later he spoke, his disquiet banished. "Well, chaps, let's review the plan one last time. Lieutenant Higgins will lead his party to the airdome so as to attack at 21:30. All aircraft on the ground will be destroyed and petrol storage tanks fired. Shoot up airdrome personnel—and any other Jerries that get in your way—and destroy or damage whatever facilities you can. Join me here at Wadi Selim not later than 22:45."

He paused before continuing with the remainder of his orders. In the uniform of a colonel of the German general staff, erect, tall and broad-shouldered, he looked Prussian rather than British. But in the hardness of his weather-worn face there were no cruel lines; and the steel-blue eyes, widely separated over a rather sharp nose, were warmed by a mouth that smiled with great ease.

"Quarles and I," he continued, "with Rumsey driving the jeep, will leave for Bardo immediately. We'll first reconnoiter the harbor and waterfront. Then we'll probably tackle the Bosche headquarters before leaving for Wadi Selim. At 22:45 we'll all leave here for our desert landing field. The transport plane that's to pick us up should be there between 23:30 and 23:45.

"Whether or not all of us are at the landing field, the plane will take off at 24:00. If we're pursued too closely we may have to signal the plane not to land; or maybe it can land and take off immediately. In any event, if some of us don't make the plane, they'll have to try and make their own way back to our lines as best they can. Are there any questions?"

The silence that settled over the group was unbroken. Then Keith spoke again.

"Set your watches. It is now eighteen thirty-nine . . . thirty-nine thirty . . . thirty-nine forty-five——"

Once more there was a pause, and the men shifted about uneasily. Abruptly Keith turned to Higgins and stuck out his hand.

"Good luck, Ned. See you later on."

"Luck, sir." Higgins' reply was low. "Take care of yourself."

Keith shook hands with all six of Higgins' group, and with each clasp he gave a bit of half-humorous advice. There was a natural reserve between them, even at this parting; but through the wall of constraint, as they exchanged comments, penetrated a sense of reciprocal respect and admiration, almost love. It was a feeling shared by those who have been through hardships and dangers together.

A few seconds later Keith climbed into the little *Volkswagen* that they had taken from the Germans on their last raid. Then, as Lieutenant Quarles settled down beside him, Keith tapped Rumsey on the shoulder and said simply, "Let's go."

Fifteen minutes of driving over the rough Libyan desert road brought them to the coastal highway. Effortlessly the little car turned onto the smooth macadam and they rolled toward Bardo. Only the rhythmic humming of the tires disturbed the night stillness; it lulled the three men to silence.

Through Keith's mind ran thoughts of the past ten days, ten days that had brought them through the last British mine field south of El Alamein to the *wadi* they had just left. It was like one long day rather than ten. All of those daylight hours under the everlasting blue of the Libyan sky and the fiery desert sun had merged into one—ten bivouacs begun in the chilly half light of dawn when camouflage nets were raised to shield men and vehicles alike from prying Axis planes; unnumbered meals, some cold, others warmed in concealed fires, but all shared with clouds of voracious flies that seemed not to care whether they feasted on man or food.

He thought, too, of those long nights of silent travel to this *djebel* country. Like the days, they fused into a single period of time, a space in which the occasional pauses, the rare engine trouble, and the daylight halts, were the only highlights. He wondered how many times he had doubted the verity of his navigational calculations and how often he had verified his course. How many hours, he asked himself, had they spent checking their maps?

His thoughts shifted to the plans they had made for this night. Did everyone understand his job? Had he neglected any details? Had he forgotten anything?

Fondly, he considered the men he had just left. He

knew them, he felt, as a father knows his children. And, like a father, he knew he would have no rest until he saw them all again. He had no doubt that they would give a good account of themselves, for he had been on raids with all of them.

Their faces flashed before his mind: Higgins, quiet, capable, red-headed Higgins, who had proved himself a dozen times over; McKenna the Scot, fierce in his hatred of everything German since that day when he had heard of his wife's death in a winter bombing; the ebullient, leathery-faced O'Meara, who laughed as he sprayed lead with his Tommy gun; Porter, who looked like a clod but whose quick thinking had saved his mates more than once; Jamison, the slim London boy who seemed so out of place in the desert yet who got along so well with the Arabs; Newberry, swearing every raid would be his last but the first to ask for new assignments. It was indeed a good crew, he told himself; and he wished he were with them instead of alone with Rumsey and Quarles.

Rumsey seemed to sense that his commander was thinking of him, for he took his eyes off the road long enough to turn his head and twist his face into that slow smile of his. He was an eager, quiet chap, sometimes too quiet, thought Keith. But at any rate, he was experienced and had proved his coolness, if not his audacity, in the last two forays.

Keith wished that he had the same confidence in Quarles that he had in Rumsey. His brow wrinkled in worry as he reflected that the youth by his side was inexperienced and untrained in the operations of the Long Range Desert Groups. This was Quarles' first raid, and Keith felt that he was certain to be much more of a liability than an asset. For the hundredth time since they had begun their trek he belabored himself for having been persuaded by the colonel to permit Quarles to come along. He had given in only because the lad spoke German so fluently—almost as well as Keith himself .

Out of the corner of his eye he glanced at Jeffrey Quarles, someday to be the eleventh Lord Crestwicke. He had to admit that the boy was rugged and physically well equipped for this type of work. The hundred and sixty pounds or so that he carried were trimly distributed over his tall frame. The squared shoulders and tapering waist set off well the uniform of a captain of the German Afrika Korps. If the face beneath that jauntily placed canvas cap had only shown some signs of maturity, Keith admitted to himself he would feel better. But the slightly turned-up nose, the clear blueness of the eyes, and the unconcerned mouth gave no evidence of the toughness that comes to the veteran only through trial by fire.

"Jerries up the road, sir."

Rumsey's words, barely loud enough to be heard above the singing tires, startled Keith. Precipitately his mind switched to the import of the warning. Every nerve and sense alert, he peered ahead. By degrees his eyes focused and he distinguished what appeared to be a roadside hut with a small group of men clustered about it. As the car gradually slowed, he made out the figures of German soldiers. Instinctively he loosened his holster, a tense, tight feeling sweeping over him. The first test was upon them.

Even before the little vehicle had rolled to a halt, a beam of light from the sentry's flashlight struck them. There was but a semblance of hesitation as the man recognized the general staff insignia. Then, without question, he saluted smartly, and waved that they could continue their way.

They were in Bardo. Slower now, the car threaded its way through the narrow streets. Surely and without error Rumsey steered his way down one quiet thoroughfare and up another; hours of patient pouring over maps had given him expert knowledge of the town. Occasionally they passed German soldiers, the gutteral conversations and clash of hobnailed boots against pavement echoing into the night as groups of two's and three's wandered aimlessly about. Only rarely did they spot the silent, robed Arab townsfolk; but the clinging, fetid odors that seemed to rise out of the ground like steam never for a moment let them forget that this was Africa.

In spite of their leisurely pace it was not long before they had traversed the width of Bardo and arrived at the breakwater which stretched out from the southern shore of the bay that had made the town a port.

Silently the car came to a halt, the low grinding of brakes lost in the crashing roar of the Mediterranean surf. Then Keith, followed by Quarles, clambered out and wordlessly waved Rumsey off to carry out the pre-arranged plan of awaiting the two officers in an alley near the German headquarters.

They stood motionless for a minute taking in the view before them. Across the mouth of the half-moon bay they saw the breakwater that extended almost to the tiny cape jutting out from the northern shore. In front of them loomed a pier warehouse and beyond, reaching like fingers into the glistening harbor waters, they could see the tips of five other wharves. The cobbled waterfront road bent with the semicircular shore, all but a small portion hidden from their view by the sharp bend it took near the second dock.

Slowly they began to walk.

As they drew closer to the first wharf a large number 6 became visible. Two small sailing ships, masts pointing skyward above the pier warehouse, lay moored to the wharf stanchions. Then in the shadows of the entrance they discerned a lone sentry standing immobile as the pier house itself. A dozen steps farther on they were challenged, then saluted and passed on as they identified themselves as "Colonel von Kalb and Captain Schmidt."

Like number six, pier five showed few signs of activity as they approached. A small coastwise freighter, apparently unloaded, sat quietly next to the warehouse. Slapping wavelets emphasized the shipboard silence. Again a single guard challenged, saluted, and permitted them to pass.

The warehouse on pier five, like the others, over-lapped from the quay onto land. As they rounded one corner of this building there came into view the re-mainder of the waterfront road. Almost as they made the turn, the moon ducked behind a cloud. Almost but not quite, the blanketing gloom shut out the sight of row upon row of vehicles. Crowding the dockside thoroughfare in the blackness, the ranks merged into shapeless lumps. Even so, a curious excitement swept over Keith at the scene and he nudged Quarles to move to the landward side of the street.

They crossed diagonally, but had not quite reached the first line of trucks when the moonlight again poured down.

"Petrol carriers!" whispered Quarles, galvanized by the revelation of the long line of gasoline tank trucks that stretched from in front of pier four as far as they could see. "What can they be doing here? Do you suppose——"

"*Sh!* Quiet, boy! That's what we have to find out," interrupted Keith. Instantly he regretted his words as out of a corner of his eyes he saw Quarles' lips tighten at the rebuke.

"Let's move along, Quarles; there's something strange about all of this," he growled more kindly.

Still walking slowly, the British officers approached

the first line of trucks. Standing silent, five in a row, and without a sign of drivers, all the trucks apparently were empty. Long hose lines, stretched out between the ranks, indicated readiness for some sort of a fueling operation.

They had moved past a dozen or so ranks before Keith spoke again: "Looks as if they're getting ready to fill up, but I don't see a sign of any tankers in the harbor or at the docks. Do you make anything of it?"

"No, sir, but we've only had a look at three piers. There may be tankers tied up at the others," said Quarles quietly.

"That's hardly possible," replied Keith. "Our air and naval reconnaissance keeps a good check on that sort of thing, and we probably would see some evidence of recent bombing here if anything had moved in within the past two weeks. We'd better move across the road again, though, and check each dock to be sure."

Quarles nodded and the two moved through the rows of trucks to the seaward side of the street. They were about to emerge from between the vehicles when Quarles pulled on Keith's coat sleeve and pointed out into the harbor.

"Look there, sir," he said.

Keith quickly turned his head.

"So," he breathed softly, "subs."

Two submarines, barely discernible, were passing through the narrow entrance between the breakwater and the north shore cape. Even as the two men watched, other subs followed. They counted a total of twelve in the harbor. Then, as the procession of submersibles seemed to end, Keith and Quarles moved out from behind the truck that had shielded them and proceeded toward the other piers.

They had scarcely taken a step when the sound of a voice, stridently piercing the silence, stopped them in their tracks. Instinctively they ducked back behind the trucks. Then, cautiously, both worked forward in the shadows of the huge vehicles toward dock number two. There they were just able to see a large group of soldiers, apparently being addressed by an officer.

Bits of phrases floated to them.

". . . docks . . . pumps . . . U-boats . . . panzers . . . first trucks fueled are to . . ."

They edged closer and the words of the speaker registered more clearly.

". . . U-boats will be moored at . . . pumps should be ready to operate by . . . o'clock. All trucks must be fueled by five A.M. They will proceed individually to the assembly points 'A' and 'B', fifteen miles and five miles, respectively, south of Bardo on the Bardo-Tobruk road. They will remain there all day in the camouflaged areas prepared. Orders for the movement forward tomorrow night will be issued at the assembly points.

"The Field Marshal himself has sent instructions from his forward headquarters that this operation must be carried out successfully if our valiant panzer divisions are to have fuel to attack. All of us must therefore leave nothing undone that will speed the operation. All must work doubly hard to see that it is carried out in the efficient manner that has already brought glory to our irresistible army."

Keith looked significantly at Quarles and nodded his head in the direction of the center of town. Like two wraiths they dodged into the shadows of the trucks. Soon they were plodding up one of the narrow side streets toward headquarters.

Tersely and somewhat as if he were thinking aloud, Keith spoke to his companion: "Here's how I figure it. The U-boats are submarine tankers. The Jerries are using them to bring in petrol to the panzers. This is the big leak that our navy and air force have not been able to plug up. The petrol carriers will fill up tonight and by dawn will be moved to two assembly points. They'll stay in those two camouflaged areas to-morrow and then tomorrow night will take the fuel to the panzer divisions. Rommel and his staff are not in Bardo. That means that we can change our plans to bomb and shoot up the Bosche GHQ. Instead we must get word to our intelligence tonight so they can send bombers here by dawn, and then scout around for those two camouflaged assembly points in daylight tomorrow and bomb them. We can't risk taking chances of not getting back, so we'll go straight to the alley and get Rumsey."

He finished speaking and as he did so became conscious of footsteps behind them. Discreetly he glanced
backward as they strode along. Two figures, though
seemingly attempting to take advantage of the shadowy street, appeared more than once in bold outline.
It was obvious that they were dogging the two Brit-
ishers, though they were making every effort not to
attract the attention of their prey.

"Quarles," Keith spoke quietly, "we're being followed. We'll keep on our way as if we didn't know
about it till I figure this thing out. Don't look back,
and for heaven's sake, don't get excited."

To his relief Keith saw that the youngster did not
so much as wince at the news. Only that same tighten-
ing of the lips marked his receipt of the information.
And that expression, the older man was sure, was only
a sign of the other's resentment of the tenor of the
warning. Again he regretted his words. They continued on their way.

A short while later he spoke again: "There's only
one thing to do. Too many soldiers in the streets and
we're too near headquarters. We can't take a chance
on luring them into an alley and slugging them. I've
got to throw them off the scent some other way. I'm
going to try a stunt at headquarters. You just carry out
what I tell you to do when we get there. Haven't time
to tell you more now."

They emerged from the side street a few feet from
the headquarters building. Boldly, though they knew

their two pursuers could not be far behind, they saun-
tered up to the entrance.

"Major Rintel is the commandant?" casually asked
Keith of the sentry after he had returned the salute.

"No, Herr Colonel, Major Mueller is our commandant. I have never heard of Major Rintel," replied
the guard.

"Ah, yes. Mueller, of course," said the British officer
as if wondering how he could possibly have failed to
remember such a simple name as Mueller. "Have the
sergeant of the guard call Major Mueller. I wish to
speak to him."

"Would not the Herr Colonel care to enter? The
major is in his office," politely rejoined the soldier.

"Have the major come out," said Keith sternly. "I
am in a hurry and must travel tonight. Schmidt,"
turning to Quarles, "have Hans bring round the
car."

Immediately the guard spoke to another soldier inside the doorway, giving the message that "a colonel
of the General Staff wished to see the Commandant
outside right away." Simultaneously, Quarles quit the
side of the pseudo-colonel to search out Rumsey and
the car.

Keith looked at his watch and, out of a corner of
his eye, toward the corner of the headquarters building near which he was sure his two trailers were lurk-
ing. He couldn't see them; but they were there, he
was sure. At any rate, he felt, Quarles would know

when he came back, for he had to pass that spot on his way to the entrance.

A short, roly-poly major bustled through the door, obviously very distressed as he tried to fasten his blouse at the same moment he smoothed his hair. He looked almost ready to burst into tears as he pulled himself up short in front of "the colonel." Clearly he was a very poor example of the race of supermen and he seemed well aware of his shortcomings.

"Good evening, Herr Colonel. Good evening, sir. I didn't know you were in this accursed town, sir. Won't you come in, sir? I assure you, Herr Colonel, my poor office is at your disposal. Won't you——" All in one breath the skittish officer spouted his words which seemed to trip over each other like little school children pouring from a classroom.

"Major Mueller!" The clipped words of the imposter were searing in tone and dammed the verbal flood of the distressed major.

"Yes, Herr Colonel?" weakly answered the other.

"I wish to speak to you. Let us move away from this door. I will speak to you in private and I cannot waste time going into this pig-pen."

"Yes, Herr Colonel. Of course, sir. As you wish, sir."

The major was now in worse shape than before. His face, which in the light streaming through the doorway had had some semblance of color, was now a pasty yellow. He twitched feverishly and scampered after

Keith like a puppy as the latter began walking to the corner.

They stopped just out of earshot of the headquarters sentry, but Keith was sure they were still within hearing distance of the two men who had been following him and Quarles. The moment they halted, Quarles drove up with Rumsey and jumped out of the car. He said only that Herr Colonel's car was ready and was motioned to silence by an imperious wave of the hand. Not unnoticed, however, was his meaningful eye movement that signaled the presence of the two pursuers in the nearby shadows.

"And now, Major Mueller," said Keith coldly, looking at the German. "You know me, of course."

"But certainly," quavered the major, uneasy but sure now that he must not confess to anything that might make him appear worse in the eyes of the visitor. "Had I known the Herr Colonel was in Bardo, I would have——"

"I did not wish my presence known," interrupted Keith with all the Prussian austerity that he could muster.

"Naturally, naturally," agreed the major, "I under——"

"But," interrupted Keith again, "I have serious charges to lodge against you, for you have failed to take proper measures to maintain the security of this port."

"Oh, Herr Colonel, that can't be, sir," expostulated

the now frightened officer in a voice that shook as it mounted in shrillness. "I have taken every possible measure—all precautions, Herr Colonel. I have guards for every warehouse on the waterfront. A motor patrol constantly goes through the town. There are foot patrols in the streets. I have done everything, Herr Colonel, I assure you—there must be some mistake, Herr Colonel—I——"

"There is no mistake, Major Mueller." Keith's words were harsh and brought the man's outflow to a halt.

"Yes, of course, Herr Colonel. What is it that the Herr Colonel finds incorrect?" The little major was not abject in his anxiety.

"The captain," motioning to Quarles, "and I have inspected the waterfront. We walked its length and were challenged by your sentries. But not once, Major, not once did your sentries make us identify ourselves. We walked through the vehicles parked on the waterfront and were not stopped. We heard an officer giving instructions to his men. We walked back to headquarters and, can you believe me, were followed by two clumsy fools who even now are trying to overhear what I am saying to you."

The scorn in the British officer's voice was searing; and as he finished he noticed what seemed to be a flurry of shadows from the direction of the corner. Apparently the two men who had trailed them had considered it better not to be found in the vicinity of the distraught major and his two important visitors. As for the major, he was completely downcast. Only a mumbled half-croak, half-squeal came from his throat.

"Ordinarily I would only reprimand you, major," said Keith in the same cold tone but now much relieved, "but in view of yesterday's intelligence warning of the expected British paratroop raid, I fear that I must relieve you of your command."

A gleam of hope darted into the major's stricken face as the import of the last few words came to him.

"Intelligence warning? But I have not received any such warning. I swear to you, Herr Colonel, that no such message was received. I——"

"What!" grated Keith in well-simulated consternation, "are you sure?"

"I swear it, Herr Colonel. I myself check every incoming message and none has been received. I will show you our files——" Breaking off in the middle of his explanations the German darted to the headquarters entrance like a scared rabbit.

More slowly the two British officers walked to the doorway as Quarles whispered, "One minute to go before the airport attack."

In a moment the major was back with a bulky message file in his hands. But now there was a note of confidence as he spoke.

"You can see for yourself, Herr Colonel. Right here, sir. You see——" He began thumbing through the file and the words poured out as fast as he could voice them.

"Of course I shall revoke my decision," said Keith reassuringly, "if I find you have not received the message. Here, Captain," he said, taking the file from the shaking hands of the German officer and handing it over to Quarles, "look through these messages and see if yesterday's intelligence warning was received. The Major and I must talk over some——"

The staccato sound of distant small-arms fire and the dull booms of explosions shattered the hush of the night. A sheet of flame reared skyward, then more thudding rumbles resounded. With a start the major yelped, "The British. Airport! Got to get troops there! Sergeant! Lieutenant Schultz!"

"Quiet, you fool. Do nothing of the sort," barked Keith as he grabbed the almost hysterical major. "That's probably only a diversion at the airport. The real attack will come on the town and waterfront. British planes are now probably near by. Order your men down to the waterfront to protect the docks and transportation. Have all anti-aircraft guns open fire and maintain it for thirty minutes. I myself will go to the airport. You stay here."

With a nod of understanding, but still screaming for the sergeant and Lieutenant Schultz, the major bounded off again. Keith and Quarles climbed into the jeep and sped off, the message file with them.

As anti-aircraft guns barked, searchlights weaved in

and out of clouds, and sirens wailed; as booming thumps and the faint crackling of rifles and machine guns floated in from the direction of the airfield, the three invaders drew near the outpost at which they had been halted on their way into Bardo. Now, though, a tremendous sheet of flame from the airdrome illumined the scene and in the light they could see at least a half dozen soldiers in the roadway.

" 'Fraid we may get into trouble if we stop this time," shouted Keith over the wind and noise. "Better take a chance on rushing 'em. Step on it as soon as they think we're about to stop," he yelled to Rumsey as he picked up a sub-machine gun from the floor of the car.

Gradually they slowed down. Then they saw the Nazi soldiers relax, sliding their cradled weapons to less ready positions. But even before they had come within a few yards of the group Quarles squeezed the trigger of the Tommy gun he held. One or two of the soldiers staggered, clutched their bodies, and slumped to the ground. The others hit the earth, ducking behind whatever cover was at hand.

In the brief interval before Keith opened fire and the jeep accelerated to full speed, Quarles caught the bitter look on his superior's face and knew he had done wrong. Then, as the bullets began chipping the ground about the flying car, he realized his blunder. In the screaming wind he heard only snatches of his commander's recriminations, ". . . should've waited

. . . too soon, dash it . . . fire before . . ."

The words faded into a groan. Then Keith lunged and toppled to the floor of the speeding car.

Numbly the youth gathered the unconscious body into his arms. Without thinking he ripped open the bloodsoaked tunic and applied a first aid compress to the torn flesh. In the darkness he could not tell how seriously Keith was hurt; he was not even certain that he was not dead.

He was sure of only one thing: he was responsible for this catastrophe. Through his blunder the Germans had been given time to fire a few well-aimed shots at the retreating car. The few seconds had made all the difference; and now Keith, who had gone through a dozen raids unscratched, was stretched out bleeding, maybe dying, maybe dead.

He was scarcely aware of the fact that they had turned off the highway onto the rougher desert road. And when they stopped, short of the wadi, it was only mechanically that he perceived Rumsey signaling with his flashlight. A few seconds later, when they had progressed the length of the ravine, the car turned off the road and halted. Then with tenderness, the two lifted the body of their chief to the ground.

In the light of a flashlight held by Rumsey, Quarles removed the compress he had applied and examined the wound. Tears of relief came to his eyes as he saw that the German bullet had been too high to be fatal. Quickly, with sure fingers, he bandaged the injury;

then they made the unconscious officer as comfortable
as they could.  Through it all, not a word was spoken.

The sound of a motor brought them to their feet
just as they were finishing with Keith.  Warily they
waited as the noise came closer.  Then the shape of
the approaching vehicle formed itself in the moonlight
and three spaced dashes of light came from it.  They
relaxed, and Rumsey flashed back the answering signal.

In a moment the truck had pulled up near them.  It
was Davis who first dismounted and reached Quarles.

"Where's the Captain?" he asked, as if unwilling that
anyone but Keith should hear this report.

"He's wounded," replied Quarles.  "Not badly," he
added as he saw the other's face fall, "but he's still
unconscious."

"We all got away," said Davis, anticipating the
officer's question, "but Lt. Higgins, O'Meara, and
Jamison were shot up.  I don't know how badly any of
them are wounded.  We were followed, too.  I don't
know how far behind us the Jerries are nor how many
of them there are.  I think we'd better move right away
and try to get to the airfield."

For a few seconds Quarles was silent as he fully
sensed the situation.  Now *he* was in command.  But
this time, he swore, he would not fail Keith and the
others.  It did not take him long to give his orders.

"Have everyone stay in the lorry, Davis," he said.
"You help Rumsey and me lift the captain into it.
Then drive as fast as you can to the landing field.  Take

off as soon as you can."

"Yes, sir," said Davis. "Will you follow in the jeep or are you coming with us?"

"No," said Quarles calmly. "No. I'm staying here. This wadi is a natural ambush and if you've been followed too closely I'll be able to delay them for a while."

Davis stood silent for a minute. Then he stuck out his hand and said, "Very well, sir. And good luck. I'll tell the captain."

"Thanks, Davis," said Quarles, "now let's get him in the lorry."

Carefully they lifted the now conscious but groggy Keith into the truck. Then Quarles walked over to the jeep that had been parked a short distance away. He was reaching into one of the compartments for some grenades when he heard the truck roar off to the airfield.

It was barely out of sight when he heard the crunch of a step behind him. He whirled about quickly, his pistol in hand.

It was Rumsey.

"What are you doing here, Rumsey?" he asked angrily. "I told Davis I wanted every man to get in the lorry and get to that plane."

"Well, sir," said Rumsey, almost self-consciously, "there's two reasons. One is that the captain sort of told me to look out for you and help you to keep out of trouble."

"I don't need your help or anyone else's," said Quarles hotly. "And I don't appreciate the fact that you have disobeyed orders that I gave. If I could, I'd send you on to the others, but I suppose it's too late for that." Rumsey's statement had done nothing to make him feel better, for now he realized that Keith had always had a low opinion of him; and his actions on the raid had certainly borne out the captain's fears.

"You haven't asked me the other reason, Lieutenant," said Rumsey smilingly as he broke in on Quarles' lugubrious line of thought.

Quarles did not answer, so Rumsey spoke again.

"The other reason is, sir, that I thought this would be the best show of the trip and I—well, I thought I'd like to be with you to see it through."

In spite of himself, his anger, and his dejection, Quarles was touched. Somehow, he felt, it couldn't be so bad if Rumsey had faith in him. And as for Keith, well, perhaps after tonight Keith would think a little better of him.

"Thanks, Rumsey," he said, without a trace of his former anger, "I'm really glad you're with me, you know. But," after a slight pause, "we've some work to do yet, so let's get started."

The plan that Quarles outlined to him was simple enough and after the two of them had loaded themselves down with grenades, Tommy guns, and plenty of ammunition, they walked back along the wadi road. Midway they parted. Quarles clambered up the side of the little ravine and continued to the entrance to place himself above that portion of the wadi road.

They didn't have long to wait.

About five minutes after Quarles had gotten himself into position he heard the sound of motors. He strained to see the number, and gradually, as they drew closer, he made out three vehicles. They were troop-carrier trucks and as they drew near the wadi they moved slowly over the rough surface.

It was all over in a short time.

Quarles simply allowed the first truck to pass, then he pulled the pin of a grenade and lobbed it toward the second truck as it drew abreast. A second and a third he hurled, then he scrambled along the side of the little gorge and heaved more grenades after the leading vehicle. Flung to the ground by the force of the first few blasts, he climbed to one knee and pressed the trigger of his submachine gun. He used it as a gardener would a hose, pointing it first in the direction of the leading truck and then spraying it over the second. To his rear he felt the concussions of the grenades that Rumsey had thrown and as he fired he heard the staccato sound of his companion's gun.

Determinedly he got to his feet and walked toward the first truck. Clip after clip he loaded, unmindful of the scattered fire that came from what remained of the leading troop carrier. He drew closer, had almost reached the bulk of the truck when he felt a searing, burning stab in his shoulder. He spun around, clutched for the air, then knew no more.

It was quiet when he regained consciousness and he was being lifted into the jeep. Dimly he saw Rumsey, felt him adjust a compress, sensed he was being placed into the seat. He realized he was wounded, somewhere near the chest or shoulder.

"Rumsey," he said weakly.

"Yes, Lieutenant," said the other, "how're you feeling?"

"A little weak," Quarles replied. "What happened?"

"We got 'em all, sir. Your first grenade landed right in the middle of the second lorry. It was a beautiful lob, sir. As good as any I've ever seen. Mine were a little short but they stopped the last one all right. I had a little trouble with some of those Jerries, but finally got 'em all."

"How about the first lorry? It was blasted wasn't it?"

"Yes, sir," said Rumsey. "Your first volley and the grenades got most of them. But one of them pinked you before I could get up to help. I finished them all off, though, Lieutenant."

Quarles felt Rumsey jab him with something. He guessed it was one of those little ampules of morphine. The jeep began rolling and the world seemed to whirl about. He fought to keep conscious and tried to speak.

"Where . . . you . . . going . . . Rumsey?" he asked feebly.

"To the desert landing field, sir. We're going to join the others," Rumsey replied.

"No . . . can't do that. I . . . told them . . . not to
. . . wait for me." He felt giddy as the sound of his
own words reached his ears.

"Yes, sir. I know you did. But you didn't say anything about not waiting for me and I told Davis we'd
be there by 24:00. And we're going to make it and
have time to spare, sir."

"Shouldn't—have done—that—Rumsey——" The
words trailed away into nothingness and he relapsed
into darkness.

The pulsing roar of airplane motors came to his ears
as he woke again. He looked up and his eyes focused
on the face of the man who was adjusting a blanket
about him. He closed his eyes again, then reopened
them. He had made no mistake, it was Keith and he
was smiling.

"How are you feeling, Jeff?" he asked.

New energy surged through him as he realized that
Keith had called him by his first name, had shown no
signs of displeasure.

"Fine, sir. How are you feeling?" he asked. "And
how are the others? Did you get word back about
Bardo? Are there——"

"*Sh!* Quiet, Jeff. One thing at a time. Everything
is all right. I just have a slight wound in my shoulder.
Guess it was the creasing I got in the head that
knocked me out. The others are okay except Higgins,
who's going to be laid up for some time. We sent
back the message by our plane wireless and unless I

miss my guess our bombers are on their way to Bardo now. What they don't get at dawn, they'll finish off in daylight tomorrow."

Quarles breathed a deep sigh.

"I'm glad, sir. But I'm sorry about Higgins. He's a fine officer and you'll miss him. I'm sorry about tonight, too. I——"

"Don't worry about tonight, Jeff. That's all right. As for Higgins, I hate to lose him, but we've found a good replacement," said Keith gently.

"You have, sir. Who is he?" asked the youth drowsily.

"It's you, Jeff. Now go to sleep. We'll be landing in a little while."

Quarles dropped off to sleep again, this time with a smile on his face.

# GIVE IT TO THEM GENTLY

by Richards Bennett

Lying in the hot sun on the top of a Philippine hill, he was reminded of that long-ago contest on a summer day that crowned a season fresh and welcome—not like this endless tropic summer. It was a day when victory in a tennis match was the biggest thing he had to fight for. And call it luck or call it his subconscious, or just call it help from home, the memory was a Godsend.

It was a tennis ball that started his memory. He had picked it up the day before, when he had gone behind the lines to have his knees dressed at an aid station. It was lying by a wreckage that once had been an officer's quarters on the old American Army post near which his regiment was now fighting the Japs. It was

an old ball, one that had probably lain there since before the war, and it would never be used on a court again; he had picked it up for his dog who had been with him all through the Philippine fighting. But when he got back to his command post in the front line there had been so much to do that he had forgotten to give the ball to Jock. Now, while he lay studying the enemy across the little valley, the ball in the pocket of his combat trousers bothered him and he dug it out to throw away.

For two days his regiment had been held up by a group of stubborn Japanese in a cave. From the low ridge on which he lay, Captain John Randolph could see the mouth of the cave; it was only three hundred yards away, on the side of a higher ridge opposite him. The cave was in a rock cliff that was almost perpendicular; it had been hewn from the solid rock by the Japs during the three years they had held the Islands. From the cave mouth downward the ground fell away so steeply that a man could climb it only with the help of hand-holds. Above, the rock face went straight up for twenty feet, then sloped steeply back a few feet to the razor edge of the ridge. The ground was covered with brown, sere grass, burnt off in spots where tracer bullets, shells or flame throwers had started grass fires.

"We'll never get them out at this rate," growled the voice of Randolph's big First Sergeant.

Randolph squinted through his binoculars. "They've got two concrete baffle walls just inside the cave entrance. That's why our charges haven't worked."

The pocket of Japs in the cave had held up the advance of the whole regiment for two days. It was easy enough to by-pass the ridge, leaving the cave and its defenders behind; but the moment they ran into resistance beyond the ridge, the enemy in the cave came out and raised havoc with light machine guns and mortars. In the daytime Randolph's men could keep the mouth of the cave covered by fire from the lower ridge, but at night they could not keep the enemy from coming out, inflicting a few casualties and scurrying back into their place of safety. Randolph had picked off a total of twelve Japs from time to time; but there might be a hundred still inside, for the other caves they had captured had been deep and long, honey-combing the whole interior of the hills. It was too dangerous to leave so many of the enemy behind as they advanced.

The cave had to be cleaned out.

Lieutenant Smith spoke to the young captain. "We've been able to get them out of every other hole with explosives or flame throwers, but this one's too hard to get at. I've tried working men up from below, but the devils toss grenades out down the slope, and I've lost two men that way. We can't get close enough to pitch our own grenades inside, even with covering fire. All they have to do is roll their eggs out from behind those baffles without ever showing a nose."

"We could shoot at them all year with machine

guns," Randolph said. "We'd have no effect on that concrete. And of course a mortar won't work on such a flat trajectory. I've sent for an anti-tank gun. It ought to be here now."

Fifteen minutes passed. The men lay sweating them out in the broiling sun. Occasional bullets whined overhead and the artillery was working hard on a section of the line to their left. Little Philippine flies swarmed on them, settling in clusters on their hands and faces. Once Randolph took a drink of almost hot water from his canteen.

"Here it comes!"

Turning, Randolph saw a group of men struggling up the slope. They were pulling by hand a fifty-seven-millimeter anti-tank gun, mounted on rubber tires. They had brought it as far as possible with a jeep, but the last part of the slope was too steep for any vehicle. When they reached the top they sank exhausted on the ground. Other artillerymen came up with ammunition, and the gun was put in place with its muzzle peeping over the edge of the ridge. The mouth of the cave was now at point-blank range.

"You can't miss from here," Randolph said to the lieutenant in charge of the gun. "Let 'er go and see what you can do to those concrete walls inside."

A shell was quickly rammed into the gun breech and a nasty crack smote the air as it was fired. There was a burst of smoke and dust against the rock cliff ten feet to the left of the cave entrance. A shrapnel fragment whined through the air. The gun aim was corrected and another fired. It hit square in the mouth of the cave.

"Give them half a dozen rounds as fast as you can go!" cried Randolph. In half a minute the rounds had been fired. There was a cloud of dust about the cave mouth now and they waited until it lifted.

"We've made a mess of that first baffle," Randolph announced, putting down his glasses. I can see the one beyond it. But they probably have a series of them all the way back. Give them another dozen and let's see what happens."

When the dust had cleared again, they saw that the first concrete wall had been reduced to rubble, and the whole cave mouth was deeply scarred. But the pile of rubble promised to block the way into the cave.

"There's a white flag!" a soldier shouted.

From behind the demolished concrete appeared the tip of a pole to which had been tied a scrap of white cloth. It was poked out tentatively, and then waved vigorously back and forth.

"I can't believe it," Randolph muttered. "Never saw 'em surrender before!" He raised his voice. "Sergeant West, take two men and go down there and get those Japs. Keep them covered all the time."

The three soldiers left the line behind the ridge and worked their way downward to the right flank. In a moment they appeared at the edge of the separating valley. They walked slowly toward the cave mouth, their weapons ready.  At the same moment, two Jap soldiers appeared in the cave mouth, crawling over the rubble pile.  They straightened up in the entrance; they were unarmed and stripped to the waist.

They could hear Sergeant West shout: "Put up your hands!" and when the enemy hands were high, his "Come down!"  The Sergeant and his men stopped and waited for the Japs to descend from the cave.

The Japs stopped as though to climb down, but suddenly they stood up again, and in perfect synchronization, their arms went back and then forward in sweeping arcs.  The Americans watching caught their breath.  They saw black objects leave the hands of the Japs, to fall, almost lazily, at the feet of Sergeant West. The Sergeant and his men had flung themselves to the ground.  The bursts of the grenades came a fraction of a second apart, two sharp cracks that split the air. Wild shouts broke from the Americans who watched and a dozen rifles and machine guns burst out at the treacherous enemy.  The Japs were already scuttling back into their hole, but one was too late.  He fell backward.  His body pitched down the slope and stopped only a few feet from the death-still figures of Sergeant West and his two men.

Beside Randolph, the First Sergeant was cursing the enemy in a frenzy of rage.  Randolph was afraid that the man would rush down in a mad attempt to storm the cave single-handed.  He gave him a low, sharp admonition.  But he too was sick with bitterness and cursed himself for sending West out to take the prisoners.

Just then he felt the tennis ball.

As he rolled toward his lieutenant, the ball got in his way against his leg. He pulled it out of his pocket and held it in his hand. He stared at it unconsciously, for his mind was working furiously to devise some new mode of attack against the cave. Moments passed before he focused his attention on what his hand was holding.

Then he remembered, suddenly, that tennis match of long ago when he had been nearly beaten by a difficulty he felt he could not overcome. He had been a First Classman at West Point, and had become a brilliant player in his last season after three years of good, but unexceptional performance. The speed and drive of his playing had won him press notice and gallery enthusiasm. At the Intercollegiate Tournament in New York he had gone through the first rounds, the quarter and semifinals, with ease, and had felt confident when he came up for the finals. His opponent was Du Maurier, a Columbia junior whose name served only to emphasize his likeness as a player to Cochet, the great French star; Du Maurier won his matches by fine tactics and skill rather than by flashing speed and overwhelming power. He forced his opponents to lose rather than forcing himself to win.

As though through the ball in his hand, Randolph saw, in an instant of embracing vision, the clay court, its lines glistening in the sun of the June day, and the gallery that watched as he and Du Maurier played the critical moment of their match.  He saw himself on the court baffled by the skill of Du Maurier's impeccable wrist that met his most vicious smashes with soft ease; half-angered by the dexterity with which the Columbia man had turned too many of his hard shots into soft pat balls that he could not return.  The score for nine games had been so even that he knew if he did not find the right return for Du Maurier's lazy, floating shots, he would lose the match.  He, the fastest collegiate player of the year, was about to be beaten by a slow ball.

He remembered vividly how the good idea had come to him as he walked back to pick up a ball that had dropped behind him and saw Captain Williamson, the Academy coach, sitting on a bench behind the court.  The captain had seemed to be speaking to him inaudibly, so that he heard again the words the coach had spoken days before, when they were discussing the tournament.

"If you ever get in a hole and you've tried every-thing—speed, drive, angle shots, precision—slow down and give it to him gently."

Give it to him gently.

That was what he had done to Du Maurier.  When Du Maurier had miraculously reached a perfect volley that Randolph had sent with all the drive of his hard, strong body, and had sent it back softly in a high and easy arch. He could have driven the ball back hard again if he had stepped close to the net. He had instead stepped to the right and taken the ball on his backhand; the ball had slid off his racket and dropped gently to the ground over the net. Du Maurier had run for it and missed and Randolph had known that he could baffle him by combining power and soft play and win the match.

That was the play of four years ago that came back to him in a flash of memory as he lay on the scorched Philippine ridge. *Give it to him gently:* was that the solution to the infinitely greater problem that confronted him now? He raised his binoculars. He laughed a little, short laugh and Lieutenant Smith beside him looked startled.

He gave his orders swiftly. "Smith, bring up a drum of gasoline. Yes, full size, one of the fifty gallon ones. Get a length of pipe. I saw some in a scrap heap down by one of the wrecked hangars. Bring it up to the end of the jeep road. I'll meet you there."

Smith's surprise did not show on his face. He said, "Right," in a matter-of-fact tone, called two noncoms to him, and started down the slope.

In another minute he was in the jeep and driving down into the valley that led to the great Luzon plain, the dust billowing around him.

It was an hour before Smith came back. Waiting for him at the bottom of the ridge, after the pitiful business of removing the bodies of West and his men,

Randolph was desperately impatient, for there was little daylight left. When the jeep drove up he leaped inside and directed them, without stopping the vehicle, down the road again and off on a little spur to the left. In two minutes they had gone to the other side of the ridge in which the cave was situated, and there they unloaded the drum of gasoline.

"This thing weighs close to four hundred pounds," Randolph said. "We've got to roll it up the slope and we've got to hurry. We'll be covered by fire so don't worry about the Japs."

If any of the others was worried about the Japs he did not mention the fact. They began to roll the heavy drum up the slope, following the razor edge. It was hard work; feeling the urgency of the time and plan, Randolph did half the work himself and exhorted the others to spurts of fierce energy. Unless the Japs came out of their caves and fired up at them, they were safe, and occasional bursts of fire from their own ridge opposite told them that any sign of enemy activity was meeting prompt discouragement. Finally they reached the top.

"Put the drum upright." With his pistol butt Randolph knocked loose the octagonal plug in the head of the drum, and unscrewed it. He took the fifteen-foot lead pipe and began to fill it with dirt scraped from the ground with his bare hands. The others added handfuls of dirt and in a few minutes the pipe was filled. Then, wedging one end of the pipe under a boulder, and levering it over another rock, he bent it slowly downward. The dirt inside the pipe kept it from collapsing at the bend. They emptied out the dirt; the pipe had been bent into an L shape, with one leg of the L much shorter than the other. Randolph jammed the short leg into the hole in the drum of gasoline, and roughly packed the joint with his olive drab handkerchief. It would leak but that wouldn't matter.

"All ready now—heave 'er over gently!"

With all the care they might have lavished on a huge china vase, they tipped the drum over on its side. The long section of pipe hung straight down over the cliff face. Peering over the edge, Randolph could see that its lower end was just above the top of the cave mouth. The red gasoline rushed through the pipe and spurted down past the entrance; the bottom of the entrance jutted out farther than the top and the thin fluid splashed onto a narrow rock ledge. Then, since the floor of the cave sloped gently downward as it went back into the hillside, the gasoline began to run into the cave.

The sloping floor was fatal for the Japanese.

The drum emptied quickly.

"That'll give 'em something to think about!" breathed Smith fiercely.

Randolph thought for a moment of the horror that must be overcoming the enemy as they saw that fearful trickle of red fluid wash into their hideout. But he remembered Sergeant West and his two murdered companions and his grim determination did not falter. He brought out his cigarette lighter.

"Stand clear!"

He twirled the wheel of the lighter and the flame sprang to life.

He lay down on his stomach and leaned his head out over the little cliff. His right hand held the windproof lighter ready to drop into the gasoline below. But before he dropped it, hesitating a last instant, he saw a figure emerge from the cave.

The enemy soldier carried another white flag. Randolph watched him with detached interest. In another moment he would start the holocaust.

While he watched, another and then another Jap came out; spellbound, Randolph stared while more than a hundred Japs poured forth. They preferred any other death to the horror of the flaming gasoline in the cave.

"Hold your fire!" Randolph shouted across the narrow valley to his company on the other side. This time they would take prisoners. They made the Japs come down from the valley to meet them, walking single file and backward, hands high and useless for treachery. When the enemy had all been rounded up and sent to the rear, Randolph himself led six men and went into the cave. Many Japanese bodies were inside, but no living person. That night there would be no shooting into their rear.

"That was a good scheme," the First Sergeant said to Randolph later. "What made you think of it?"

"We hit them hard and didn't get anywhere," Randolph answered. "So I decided to give it to them gently. I thought maybe they wouldn't be able to stand it."

# HARD-LUCK REGIMENT

## by William Chamberlain

It was a little after 0400 when Major Clay Daggett came back to the Command Post after walking the perimeter where his first battalion—what was left of it—huddled in its foxholes. The November fog held the Abenschendt ridge in clammy fingers; through the fog, rain drizzled steadily. It was getting colder and presently the rain would turn to snow.

That would be just another misery for the beaten, unhappy men clinging to the semiperimeter around this ruined town, Clay thought tiredly. Just more of the sort of thing you could expect when you were part of a regiment which had worn the "hard-luck" tag ever since World War I. Clay Daggett had joined the regiment a scant ten days ago, but already its jinx had begun to ride his shoulders.

He had still been a stranger to most of the outfit when they jumped off into the dripping green horror of the Huertgen Forest—a wilderness of steep gorges and tangled ravines guarded by the tall firs that brooded somber as German legend. It had been only four days earlier that he had reported in to regiment; he had been fresh from the States with his major's leaves still shiny new. The regiment's Commanding Officer was a hard-rock colonel named Dan Sharkey, a small, rawhided man who'd come up from the ranks and who dyed his hair to hide his fifty-six years. He had fixed young Clay Daggett with stony, gray eyes.

"Another Pentagon soldier," he had said in a harsh greeting. "You'll find things different up here, Major."

A thread of anger had run in Clay for a moment. He was a tall, lanky officer with fair hair and a handsome face that reddened too easily. It had started to get red, then—he had not asked to be stuck at a desk through two years of war as this hatchet-faced old man, with the noncom marks still on him, seemed to think!

"I expect it to be different, sir," he said. "I asked to come to this regiment."

The gray light had changed a little in Dan Sharkey's eyes.

"Why?" he had demanded in his rasping voice. "Are you stupid, Major? Don't you know that this is a hard-luck regiment? Don't you know that it wears a jinx around its neck?"

"I know about the regiment, sir," Clay had retorted

angrily, checking himself as he'd started to add that any regiment was only as good as its commander. He added, instead, "I don't believe in hard luck, Colonel. I don't believe in jinxes, either."

Oddly enough, that had seemed to pacify old Dan Sharkey a little, because he had growled, "Neither do I, Major. I'm sending you to Smith as exec. of the first battalion. Keep your nose clean."

Clay hadn't given old Dan Sharkey the real reason he had asked to come to this regiment. It was a sentimental reason—one that that old buzzard with his phony black hair would never understand. It was just that the Daggetts, when they had gone to war, had always fought in this regiment. Clay's great-grandfather had been with the regiment when the gray waves of Pickett's charge had rolled up Cemetery Ridge against it at Gettysburg; Clay's father had fought with this regiment in the Argonne.

Now, as he came back to his CP in the cold hour before dawn, Clay Daggett was wondering if he'd been wrong in saying that he didn't believe in hard luck. Because after four days of German counterattack, it looked as though the regiment might die before another night settled down here on the Abenschendt-Kolm ridge.

They had jumped off five days before and the first day's fight hadn't been too bad. The regiment, leaving its second battalion to guard its north flank, had sent its two other battalions in column down the Zweibrau

Trail, third battalion in the lead and first following. They had slithered through the mud of the steep, winding trail—which now was their only link with division—forded the swiftly rushing Zweibrau Wehr and started their slow climb out of the gorge to the two towns on the Abenschendt-Kolm ridge.

First battalion had been in Abenschendt by dark that night; third battalion had reached Kolm, the regimental objective, a mile further along the road to the southeast. The Germans had been caught off balance and resistance had been light, but the enemy had reacted later with swift violence. That night Abenschendt—the twenty-odd deserted houses sitting vacant-eyed astride the road to Kolm—had taken a brutal shelling; with first light the next day, German armor and infantry had come surging in with counter-attacks that had been increasing steadily in weight and viciousness. The Roer dams lay vulnerable behind these two villages on the ridge, and the Germans did not mean to give them up.

Colonel Smith had died of wounds near the evening of the second day, and Clay Daggett, in his first fight, succeeded to command of the battalion. For two more endless days he'd clung to his perimeter here, while casualties mounted and ammunition ran low because the weasels—tracked supply-vehicles that tried to come along the almost-impossible Zweibrau Trail—were either destroyed by shellfire or threw their tracks or fell off into the gorge. Since day before yesterday, the first and third battalions had been orphans on the ridge.

And now the first battalion was an orphan here alone, because the third had been kicked out of Kolm yesterday afternoon—shot to pieces, with the battalion commander dead and the rest of the battalion broken into little knots of beaten and scared men. They had been drifting back into Abenschendt during the night, taking refuge in the town's cellars or slogging along, heads down, toward the rear. No longer soldiers; just tired, whipped men. So Clay's somber thoughts ran.

The CP was in the cellar of a blasted house, crouched at the edge of what once had been an orchard before the shells had scythed-down most of the trees. Most of that shelling had died away for a little while now—only an occasional round crumped down to send its wicked "varoooom" through the town. *Just enough to keep tired men awake and uneasy in their holes,* Clay thought bitterly.

He went down the broken steps and past the blanket that was hung as a door. A lantern dripped sickly light across the cellar. There were a table with a map and a couple of stools and a field telephone standing on an ammunition box.

Master Sergeant Ed Feldstone, acting as telephone guard, got up from the table as Clay came in. Ed Feldstone had worn the Army's cloth for a long time now—he'd already had ten years of service behind him when he'd fought with the regiment back in the 1918 war. A sober, grizzled man.

"Everything quiet, Sergeant?" Clay asked. His voice was curter than he'd meant it to be—he liked Ed Feldstone. "Any messages come down from regiment?" he added more civilly.

"Yeah to both, Major," Feldstone said. "We got orders to jump off at 0800—the Old Man wants Kolm back."

Clay turned his head slowly and stared back at Ed Feldstone with eyes that held incomprehension for a moment; then his face began to get red. "Did you say 'orders to attack,' Sergeant?"

Feldstone nodded and began to make a cigarette out of brown paper and sack tobacco. "That's right, Major," he murmured. "The colonel is on his way here now. We attack at 0800."

The flush deepened in Daggett's thin face. "The man's stark, raving crazy!" he said violently. Then he stopped and recovered his temper with an effort—you didn't gripe about orders to your noncoms. He added more quietly, "Forget that I said that, Feldstone. You think you could get some hot coffee somewhere?"

"Yeah," Feldstone said. "I'll be back."

He went on out, thinking as he started into the fog: *The boy's right about this—Dan is off his nut if he thinks that we've got anything left here in this stinking town to attack with.* But if Dan Sharkey said they'd attack, they'd attack—even if there was nothing but a squad left to follow Dan into Kolm. Sergeant Ed Feldstone had soldiered with old Dan Sharkey for a long time now. The two had been noncoms together in this regiment back in 1918.

Clay Daggett sat tiredly down on the stool after Feldstone had gone; he propped his elbows on the table and stared at the acetate overlay which covered the map. The overlay was marked with small symbols to show where the battalion lay—Clay needed no map to tell him that. He could close his eyes and see the foxholes where bearded, muddy men, starved for lack of sleep, had been crouching as he'd walked the perimeter an hour ago. Men, too few of them now, with their ammunition belts almost empty and nothing but guts left to meet the fury of the German armor.

Attack! That was a laugh!

Boots scraped on the stone outside, but Daggett, busy with his grim thoughts, didn't look up. It would be Ed Feldstone coming back with the coffee, he guessed, and suddenly he didn't want any coffee—why should he be sitting here drinking hot coffee when the men had no coffee out there in the foxholes?

"Put it down, Sergeant," he said. "I've changed my mind."

It wasn't Sergeant Ed Feldstone—it was Dan Sharkey, shoving the blanket impatiently aside and coming on into the cellar. The yellow light of the lantern washed across the old man's flinty face as Daggett got slowly to his feet.

"Did you get my attack order, Major?" Sharkey

snapped. "I saw little sign of it outside, if you did! Stragglers all over the place! Why?"

The words caught Clay off balance as he felt resentment run through him. It wasn't fair. "Sir," he said, "those are men from the third battalion. They've been drifting back here since dark. They're not my men."

Old Dan Sharkey stalked across to stand in front of the table, his muddy overcoat pushed back and thumbs hooked in his pistol belt while he glared at Clay. "What difference does it make whose men they are?" he demanded in a voice edged as torn tin. "They've got two arms and two legs and they can shoot, can't they? Use 'em to fill up your companies, man! Do I have to tell you that?"

Clay felt a little thread of confusion run through his tired mind—he should have thought of that, he guessed. He'd just considered that those men belonged to someone else; that someone else had the responsibility for them. Beyond the colonel's slight figure he saw Ed Feldstone come back through the door with two canteen cups of coffee in his big hands. The steam rose in the cold air.

"I guess I didn't think of that, Colonel," he heard himself saying. "I had no authority . . . the men didn't belong to me. . . ." The angry glare in Sharkey's eyes was like a slap across Clay's face.

"Major," Sharkey was saying, "in war you do what has to be done, authority or no authority! In a little while now enough Kraut armor will be coming up at us out of those draws to gobble the last of this regiment up. There's only one thing we can do about it! Beat them to the punch! Do you get that?"

Clay said, "Yes, sir," in a hoarse voice, badly shaken now.

"Then get out there and start kicking men out of holes and putting them into your rifle squads, man! Do I have to lead you by the hand? This regiment is going back into Kolm and, when it goes, every man that can so much as crawl is going with it!"

Clay said, "Yes, sir," again in a dead voice and picked up his helmet as he moved toward the door. His hand was on the blanket when Sharkey's voice halted him again.

"I'll be out on the perimeter in a half hour, Major, to see how you're doing. Pass the word to your company commanders that I'll issue the attack order here at 0700. All of you will be here!"

When Daggett had gone, Feldstone brought the two steaming canteen cups to the rickety table and put them down beside the map. "No need to waste good Java," he grunted. "Get that coffee into your belly, Dan. It'll do you good. You were pretty rough on the boy."

When the two of them were alone, Ed Feldstone didn't bother to stand on ceremony with Dan—they'd known each other too long. Sharkey sat on the stool Daggett had vacated.

"Because I was, maybe he'll still be alive tomorrow

morning," he said grimly. "Well, don't stand there with your finger in your mouth, Ed. Spit it out! You think I'm crazy to talk about an attack!"

"Yeah," Ed Feldstone said thoughtfully. "I guess I do, Dan. We ain't got very much left to attack with—no tanks, no artillery, the ammo's about run out. . . ."

"We've got the fog, Ed," Dan said.

Feldstone looked back at the other with puzzled eyes. "Yeah," he said. "We got the fog—I wish somebody else had it."

Sharkey gulped a long swig of the hot coffee, put the canteen cup down and his voice was milder now. "Ed," he said, "can you think back about twenty-six years? If you can, maybe you remember how a whole division marched right through the middle of the German lines one night in 1918. When morning came, there they were sitting on the Krauts, and the war was over."

"Yeah," Feldstone said dryly. "It was the prize foul-up of that war, as I remember."

"It worked," Dan Sharkey said harshly. "It worked because the Krauts weren't expecting that anyone would pull such a fool trick. Well, it's going to work for us! Only we'll use the fog. At 0800 what's left of this regiment is going to form up on the road. Then we're going to march back down the middle of the road to Kolm. When we get there, we're going to stay this time, Ed!"

Ed Feldstone allowed his breath to go out in a faint sigh as he started to build another cigarette for himself. "It's crazy, Dan," he said finally.   'They'll hang you for it back at division if the Krauts don't kill you first.  But I reckon I'll go along."

"Maybe they'll hang me, maybe they won't," old Dan said violently. "If we get back into Kolm the Krauts will no longer have direct artillery observation on the river road.  Division can open it up then—get ammo and supplies up here to us.  Help—if we need it, Ed."

"Yeah," Feldstone said.  "If we get Kolm an' hold onto it.  If we don't we're all dead, Dan."

"What do you want to do—live to be a hundred?" Sharkey asked sourly.  "I'm going out to see how Daggett is doing!"

Sergeant Ed Feldstone finished his coffee, staring moodily at the map after Dan Sharkey had gone. There was just a chance—a wee, small chance—that Dan might get away with this, Feldstone was thinking. Dan was a tough rooster—always had been.  Feldstone's mind drifted back to that day in 1918 when a battalion of this regiment had come out of the Argonne with two-thirds of its rifle strength gone and a sergeant commanding it because all of its officers were casualties.  Old Dan Sharkey—it had been young Dan then— had been that sergeant.  So Ed Feldstone knew the affection that Dan had for this hard-luck regiment— Dan would not sacrifice it unless he felt that it had a chance.  So the crazy scheme might just work.

The *burr* of the field phone broke into Feldstone's

thoughts and he reached for the handset, identified himself and recognized the voice at the other end. It was Heine Schmidt, the message-center chief at the command post of the regiment's rear echelon still north of the Zweibrau Wehr. "I got a message for the colonel," Schmidt said. "He there, Ed?"

"He ain't here," Feldstone said. "Give me the message, Heine. I'll see he gets it."

"Like you seen that I got back that ten bucks you owe me," Schmidt said sourly. "You can't hide up there in the boondocks forever, you debt-dodger. Well, I got news for you—you're working for a buck general now. How do you like them apples?"

"Never mind the clowning," Feldstone said. "Just give me that message. I got better things to do than beat my gums with the lousy rear echelon."

"I ain't kidding you," Schmidt told him. "Radio just come from division. It says Dan's promoted to buck general and for him to turn command over to the next senior officer and shag back to the division CP. The regiment's being pulled back across the Zweibrau tonight, since it seems you birds up there can't take Kolm anyway."

"I don't believe it," Feldstone said flatly, his mind still on the first part of the message. "Why would anybody want to ruin a good colonel by puttin' a star on him?"

"I wouldn't know," Schmidt grunted. "But I got an idea you can use. Get old Iron Pants to make you his aide—then you can come back with him and pay me that ten bucks."

Feldstone heard Schmidt's snicker as he cut off. *Well, now that is a switch,* he thought as he put the handset down. *Usually, you get your regiment shot up and you find yourself back in Paris counting blankets and beans. You don't get a star pinned on you—not even a buck general's star. Maybe the division commander we got ain't as dumb as I thought. I better go tell Dan.*

It was a little before 0700 when Dan Sharkey got back to the CP in the smelly cellar and went in through the blanket door. A lieutenant that Dan didn't know was bending over the map on the table and making new marks on the acetate overlay. He straightened as he saw the older man come into the light.

"Sir," he said, blinking, "I didn't know the colonel was up here. Major Daggett's out on the perimeter somewhere and ——"

"Let it go," Dan Sharkey said gruffly. "Think you can rustle me up a coffee somewhere, son? I'm getting too old to be paddle-footing it around in the rain."

The lieutenant grinned faintly and said, "Yes, *sir!* I'll get some coffee," and went on out thinking: *With the Old Man up here things are going to pop today, I'll bet. I feel good he's here, though.*

He came back with the coffee after a little, and Dan growled his thanks. Daggett and his company commanders would be here soon. Young Daggett hadn't done too bad a job in getting the battalion reorganized, he decided. The boy would probably make a good troop leader one day.

Boots, scraping against the stone beyond the blanket, told him that they were coming now and he put the canteen cup away and got to his feet. "Come on in!" he snapped.

They came with Clay Daggett in the lead, his company commanders behind him—all of them muddy and with the whipped look showing in their drawn faces. Dan's thin mouth tightened. He had seen that look on men's faces before. It wasn't going to be easy to take what was left of the hard-luck regiment back into Kolm. For a moment he stood there, putting his hard stare onto each of them.

"Gentlemen," he said then, biting at his words, "this is going to be a short field order—you will not need to take notes. At 0800 the regiment will attack in column down the Kolm road. It is now 0710—set your watches. I will move at the head of the column. Are there any questions?"

The shocked silence that greeted his words could be cut with a knife, he thought absently. Ed Feldstone had come into the cellar now and was making frantic gestures from where he stood behind the others. Well, Ed would have to wait because it looked as though Major Clay Daggett had something to say—all of the color had gone out of the younger man's face, leaving it a dirty gray.

"In column down the Kolm road, sir?" he said in a shocked voice: "That's suicide! We wouldn't have a chance!"

Sergeant Ed Feldstone was pushing forward now, coming up to the table to stand close to Dan. He made his voice a hoarse whisper, but his words carried into the close room.

"I been trying to find you, Dan," he said urgently. "The attack's off—division says we're to pull back across the Zweibrau tonight. Orders are you're to turn over command to the next senior officer an' report back to the division CP right away——"

Daggett's voice, suddenly relieved, cut off Feldstone's words. "I am the next senior officer here, Colonel Sharkey. I'm sorry, but I'll take the regiment back across the river tonight."

For a moment Dan stood there looking back at the other, his face settling into harder lines. But, when he spoke, his voice was almost kind—as though he spoke to a child who didn't understand.

"By tonight, Major," he said, "there will be no regiment left to take back. The attack orders stand—we jump off in just forty minutes. That is all, gentlemen."

"No!" Daggett said violently, color flooding into his gray face now. "You've butchered this regiment, Colonel. Being relieved and sent to the rear is the price you're paying for that! I'm taking command as of now—there will be no attack!"

"Major," Dan said, still with that terrible softness in his voice, "we move down the Kolm road at 0800. Argue any more about that and I will stand you in front of a wall and shoot you!"

Stark silence hung again in the smelly air of the cellar as the officers in front of Dan avoided one another's eyes. Then Ed Feldstone said heavily, speaking as though he and Dan were alone now, "You ain't being relieved to go back and count beans in Paris, Dan. They're pinnin' a star on you."

"What difference does that make in anything?" Dan demanded harshly. "Get back to your commands, gentlemen!"

The company commanders filed out. Clay Daggett hesitated for a moment, an unbelieving look in his eyes. Then he shook his head and turned and followed the others.

Dan Sharkey reached down and picked up his helmet from the floor; he jammed it down over his ears as he gave Feldstone a hard look.

"I ought to tack those stripes of yours up on the barn door," he said sourly. "Find me a carbine somewhere —then form the command group up and wait for me at the head of the column, Ed."

Ed Feldstone knew that this was no use but he might as well make the try. "Dan," he said, "why can't you stay back where you belong? I'd like to be able to tell my grandkids that I once hobnobbed around with a live general."

"You got no grandkids that would own up to you,"
Dan grunted with a note of affection in his voice. "Get
going, Ed."

The sky was a dirty gray and the rain was snow now
—fat flakes drifting down like the petals of white
roses. Fog closed off the rest of the world as the word
passed and the regiment began to leave its holes and
form up on the road. Men moved with the unprotest-
ing obedience of automatons—not surprised, not
angry. Anything was better than to lie beneath the
weight of the German counterattacks for another endless day. Anyway, this was the hard-luck regiment.

The command group came out of the fog, boots
making a hollow clump against the cobbled road. Clay
Daggett, his head fuzzy with the events of the last
hour, came up as Feldsone halted his little party at
the head of the forming column.

"Where's the colonel?" Clay asked.

"He'll be along," Ed said.

"He must hate this regiment," Clay said as though
he spoke to himself.

"Major," Feldstone murmured softly, "Dan Sharkey
is proud of this regiment—he's felt every bullet it's
taken in this fight. That's the reason he's taking it
back to Kolm. He figures this regiment belongs to him
ever since that day he brought one of its battalions
out of the Argonne twenty-six years ago. Dan was a
sergeant then."

Clay Daggett started a little and an odd expression

came into his face. He had heard of that; his father
had told the story a thousand times, always ending
with:

"That sergeant was the best soldier I ever saw, Clay.
I never learned his name."

"That was Dan Sharkey?" Clay asked.

"That was Dan," Ed Feldstone said.

Then Dan Sharkey came tramping out of the fog
and took his place at the head of the column, a sal-
vaged carbine slung from his shoulder. "Come on,"
he growled. "What are you waiting for? An engraved
invitation?"

This was crazy and it wasn't war! A phalanx of
muddy, red-eyed men had risen out of the ground and
was marching down to Kolm—a ghost army moving
through the fog. And presently the sheer insanity of
it—its bravado and its mad audacity—began to infect
the column with an excitement that was heightened
by memory of the misery in the foxholes that had been
left behind.

This was the hard-luck regiment, was it? This was
the regiment that wore a jinx around its neck? Well,
try this on your fiddle, bud! How many other regiments have stood up on their hind legs and have
marched smack into the middle of the Kraut army?
How many other regiments have got a tough old
rooster like Dan Sharkey marching with them? And
the old buzzard a general now—for the word of that
had passed along the grapevine.

Spud Haskins, a BAR man marching in Able Company just behind the command group, put that into words above the tramp of boots which was beating out a steady "slap-thud" now. "Who'd ever thought this lousy outfit would rate a general for a C.O.?" he asked, and his words carried up to Clay Daggett, stumping along beside Ed Feldstone. "Maybe we ought to pass in review for him."

"Never mind about passing in review," a sergeant named Kovacs answered roughly. "You're passing in review now up on your way to Kolm. Pick up the step, boy! Hup, two, three, four!"

A snicker started and ran back down the column and presently the song started—not loud at first but growing louder, until Clay felt it blowing on the back of his neck as he marched into the fog. A fighting man's song that had been born of another war.

> *The general got the Croix de Guerre,*
> *Parley-voo. . . .*

The chant grew, swinging in time to the stamp of boots and the creak of gun slings. The hard-luck regiment flinging its defiance into the teeth of the world. And Clay Daggett, hearing it, knew that this was a hard-luck regiment no longer; that this had never been a hard-luck regiment at all.

> *Oh, the general got the Croix de Guerre,*
> *And the son-of-a-gun was never there,*
> *Hinky dinky parley-voo.*

So, the hard-luck regiment went back into Kolm on a foggy November morning and it took the town again without firing a shot because panic—the deadliest of an army's enemies—seized the town's defenders and they fled as they heard the crazy singing and heard the solid tramp of a ghost army coming at them out of the fog. Presently the Germans came back, but it was too late now—the regiment had found itself. It had its tail up and it fought with cold ferocity.

It was near 1530 when the heaviest German attack came in. The rocket-launcher teams, burning up the last of their rounds, stopped the German tanks cold, but the German infantry—S.S. troops and hard-fighting men—surged forward in a final desperate bid for Kolm. They penetrated to the town's edge and there old Dan Sharkey, already twice wounded, met them at the head of the counterattack that he personally led.

Men fought there, growling deep-throated curses and killing with naked steel and with rocks and with bare hands. But the Germans could not match the savage fury of the regiment now, and presently this attack, too, began to ebb toward the woods looming dimly through the fog and the falling snow. The regiment still owned the town, but it had paid a price. Ed Feldstone had taken the bullet that had waited for him for twenty-six years. Old Dan Sharkey had been burp-gunned through the belly—Clay had seen him go down.

Now that the town was clear once more, Clay came

back, dodging the shellfire which was crumping down to cover the German withdrawal. He brought Dan with him, carrying the older man tenderly in his arms. A hasty aid station had been set up in another smelly cellar in another ruined house and Clay left old Dan there, then went back to the street where the shells were falling faster now.

He was in command.

Two more attacks came in before the afternoon began to die, but they were weaker—not pressed home as the earlier ones had been. By 1700, with dark coming down and the snow still falling, Clay sent a radio message to division that the regiment had Kolm and that the river road could be opened. Got word back that ammunition and food and help were on their way. He carried that word to Dan Sharkey, lying in the cold cellar with the rest of the wounded.

Dan still lived, grunted as Clay gave him the message. His eyes were flinty as ever as he stared up, but a faint satisfaction eased the deep lines of his leathery face.

"The regiment's yours now, boy," he said, the familiar rasp still in his voice although his words came more slowly now. "You're doing okay. Not bad, to go from battalion exec. to regimental commander in five days' time. No, not bad."

"Not as good as from platoon sergeant to battalion commander, sir," Clay said gently and saw Dan's eyes soften.

"So you know about that," he murmured. "I'm turning a good regiment over to you, Major. A good regiment."

Clay could think of no answer to that. He blinked and frowned and put a hand on Dan's shoulder. "Division radioed 'Well done,' sir," he said huskily. "The division commander says for you to get back there before you get your fool self killed."

Dan Sharkey thought of that for a moment, the light falling across the gullies of his face. Then his lips twisted into a tight grin that did not hide the pain running in him.

"Tell him nuts, boy," he said, so low that Clay barely heard the words. "Who ever heard of a dead general?"

Presently Clay got back to his feet and went on into the deepening night. Falling snow was soft against his face as he turned toward where his makeshift CP lay. He had left something of himself behind in that cellar, he knew. He would never be quite the same again. Off somewhere a man was singing softly:

> *Oh, the general got the Croix de Guerre,*
> *The son-of-a-gun was everywhere,*
> *Hinky dinky, parley-voo.*

# THE CHROMIUM LADDER
by John B. Stanley

Hutton-Haring was happy. There was, he felt, every reason to be happy, for today everything seemed just right. There was his Spitfire, for instance, smoothly slicing the crisp spring air along with the others of C Squadron. It seemed to roar with the same sense of elation that filled its pilot. Then there was the weather —so perfect that only wispy clouds floated between the metallic, sun-glittering sheen of the English Channel and the sleek warplanes twenty thousand feet above it. Finally there was the mission: to sweep the skies of any Nazi fighters that might rise above the coasts of France to intercept the American bombers that soon would be speeding eastward. Most of all he was happy about the mission of his squadron, for the briefing had indicated that there was a very good chance of action. And action was exactly what Dennis Hamilton Hutton-Haring craved most.

"I've a private score to settle with Jerry, y'know," he had said to Pat Fowley just that morning, "and I mean to settle it today if only one bloody Nazi plane takes the air!"

He had been saying almost the same thing each day for a month, ever since that first encounter with the enemy when bad luck had lost him a victory and had almost cost him his own plane. But a month of routine patrolling had been fruitless, had resulted in nothing but a burning desire to even things up with the Luftwaffe.

For a moment, as there flitted through his mind the possibility that even today he might not succeed, a frown clouded the bright blue eyes and swept across his face. He took a fierce, quick swipe at his blond toothbrush mustache. Then his mouth became amiable again and the wrinkle in his long pointed nose disappeared. He would, he *must* meet and beat a German today, he told himself.

He searched the skies carefully, not forgetting to cast frequent wary glances rearward, for in today's flight he was "Tail-end Charlie," charged with protecting the squadron from attack in the rear. With disappointment he noted no sign of the enemy. He looked around at the other ships in the squadron. The lead plane, Manning's, was changing direction and the

formation was beginning a long, lazy swing north-
ward, the first lap in its homeward journey. He wondered if the bombers were on time and lifted his eyes
to see. They were. Ten thousand feet above him sped
a huge fleet of Flying Fortresses, their vapor trails like
sky-writing, spelling out the doom they were taking
to the continent. The sight fascinated him and for a
moment he forgot his own part in the drama that was
unfolding.

"Bandits at eleven o'clock! Fifteen thousand!"

The voice of Squadron Leader Manning crackled
over the earphones and jolted him out of his trance.
Quickly as the words died away Dennis glanced to his
left front. Five thousand feet below he saw the Nazi
Messerschmitts. They were flying south and outnum-
bered the RAF formation by almost two to one.

"All set, chaps? There's what we've been looking
for," said Manning coolly, over the radio. "Let's give
it to them. Tally-ho!"

"Tally-ho!" yelled Dennis exultantly. Close on
Fowley's tail, he followed the plane ahead as it dove
toward the German craft.

Like plummeting meteors, the Spitfires plunged
downward. Too late, almost as the leading planes were
upon them, the Nazis became aware of the attack and
attempted to climb. But by then jets of tracers were
pouring into the formation and, in a breathless second, two of the black-crossed ships were flaming, then
furiously smoking, then wabbling queerly earthward.

Another moment and the ranks of the Luftwaffe array had been shattered. Now the skies were filled with an unmarshaled swarm of aircraft.

Dennis, paired with Fowley and still hanging on his tail, found himself making a sharp banking turn to the left in the direction of three Nazi planes that were beginning a climb. The Germans were caught completely at a loss. As Fowley's bursts poured into the second plane, Dennis sighted his guns at the third. An instant later he pressed the gun button on his control stick and saw the converging leaden streams rip into the belly of the enemy craft. There was a blinding flash. Then only bits of debris filled the skies where once had been a Messerschmitt. Dennis had scored.

It was the shock of the explosion more than the pleasurable surprise that followed the disintegration of the German plane that confused Dennis. He threw up his hands as if to ward off the flying fragments, and instinctively sheered his ship from the blast. When he regained his calm, only a few seconds later, he discovered he had lost Fowley.

Dennis looked about. All around him was conflict: Spitfires driving, climbing, and furiously tearing into the enemy; Messerschmitts lunging in all directions and attempting to press home their numerical advantage; tracers carving paths in all quarters. Through it all, somehow, he finally spotted Fowley, but even as he watched him pour fire into an enemy that was using every evasive trick to get out of the Briton's gunsights, another Nazi ship came from nowhere to attack his partner from behind.

"Careful, Pat," breathed Dennis into the microphone, "there's a tailpecker after you!" Then pushing the throttle forward, he whirled into position to put himself behind Fowley's attacker.

Loops piled upon rolls and rolls upon loops as the four planes tossed about in the skies. Desperately each pursuer hung onto his prey, seldom managing to get in bursts of fire but unwilling to break from the engagement. Finally Fowley's stalker, in a half-roll and dive designed to ensnare Hutton-Haring, gave up his quarry. Grimly Dennis hung on, and as he darted after the Messerschmitt he found opportunity to let go a short burst of fire. Once again he saw his bullets chew up a German fuselage. Great chunks flew off and went hurtling past.

Then it happened.

A series of clanging metallic bangs jarred his eardrums, and a row of large holes punctured the starboard wingtip, then swept straight inboard to the fuselage. Even in the split second that it took, he watched each perforation individually materialize. He turned his head just in time to see the blazing guns of another Nazi that had jumped him. A deafening crash shook the Spitfire and everything went black.

Coming out of the darkness that had engulfed him, he found his plane hurtling downward. Black gradually turned to red and he dimly perceived the nose of the plane pointing toward a hazy maroon sea. Seconds later he was almost normal and with a curious lethargy attempted to pull the plane out of its dive. It was mushy and sluggish, so he knew the elevators had been hit, but slowly it leveled off.

Then for the first time he noticed the tiny flames that were licking their way toward him from over the engine cowling. He shook his head groggily. The redness had faded out and colors were true again. The sea, a thousand feet below, was blue green; the flames moving closer were reddish orange; the smoke pouring more thickly into his face was grayish black. He looked around above and beneath him. Then he released the catch on the escape hatch and saw it arch off to the sea. The air seemed to clear his head and he turned the radio switch to "transmit."

"Cheerio, Dabney," he said after giving the call signal, "I've come a cropper over the Channel. Near the French coast. I'm bailing out."

He worked rudder and stick until the Spitfire wobbled lazily over onto its back. Still a trifle groggy, he hung suspended for a moment and thought of how queer it seemed to see Channel waters instead of blue skies rushing past his gaze. Then he gave himself a slight push and like a deadweight shot earthward out of the cockpit.

For a brief instant he knew panic, but the jerk of the opening parachute jarred him loose of his apprehensions. His descent became gentle and, as he oscillated at the whim of the silken cap above him, he became almost cheerful. This, he told himself, was much better than a crash landing in a flaming plane. He breathed a prayer of thanks and looked toward the sea.

The Channel appeared less and less inviting as it drew near. The water seemed to be rushing toward him much more rapidly than it should. He glanced about for a sight of surface craft, or signs of his former companions. Nothing but water and clear skies. His previous cheerfulness was replaced with misgivings. The closer he came to the choppy waves, the faster he seemed to fall. He checked his Mae West nervously to make sure it was properly inflated. With fumbling fingers he grasped the release catch that would free him from his chute. He stared at the water fixedly and, hypnotized by the speed with which he was descending, froze his grip on the shrouds of the parachute. Fifty feet above the waves he sucked in a gulp of air, held it, and steeled himself. Then with an awkward splash, he plunged into the Channel.

He was coughing salty spume, gasping and choking as he came to the surface. To his surprise he found himself still clutching the cords of his parachute. It was even more astonishing, though, to note the ease with which he was remaining afloat. Under water for only a brief moment, he realized that the grasp he had maintained on the shrouds had been a stroke of luck, for a pocket of air had gathered under the silk. Not only had it retarded his plunge but now, like a huge white cork, the parachute was bobbing on the surface. He tightened his grasp.

The water was cold and not nearly so placid as it had looked from the air. Supported though he was by his Mae West and aided by the buoyant chute, he pitched about, shipping a great deal too much sea. And with each mouthful of English Channel that he spat out, he called down imprecations upon the Luftwaffe. His wrath mounted gradually.

Between spasms of indignation, he took stock of his predicament. He had noticed during his descent that he was much closer to the enemy-held French coast than to England. Air-sea rescue craft, he knew, were operated by both the RAF and the Germans. Both sides, he also knew, would have boats out searching for downed pilots. The big question was whether rescue would come at the hands of a British patrol or from the enemy. Then, as a particularly vicious wave struck him, he decided that he didn't care who saved him, friends or foes, as long as some one came soon.

One thing gave him hope: the parachute to which he still clung with nearly frozen hands. The billowing silk should loom prominently on the surface and attract searchers. Though the chances were that his proximity to France did not favor his being picked up by a British craft, he decided to be philosophical about it.

The hour that followed seemed like the better part of a day and his philosophy wore very thin. More than once he wondered why he had ever felt any liking for the sea or anything connected with it. Several times he told himself that he had been a fool to bail out of his flaming ship. Finally an unruly wave tossed him about and the last vestiges of his patience disappeared. With all the breath he could gather into his tired lungs he heaped abuse upon the Royal Navy, the RAF sea patrols, the Luftwaffe, and the world in general. The shouting made him feel better.

A screaming whistle and a crash of shellfire abruptly silenced him. Another whistle and crash, then a third followed. He was perplexed until it dawned upon him that shore batteries were firing in his general direction; then he exploded in vituperation at an enemy who would fire at such a target. Anyone who would shoot artillery at a poor bloke floundering in the sea deserved the worst, he reflected. He promised himself he would pay them back next time he took to the air.

"There he is, sir!"

The voice came from nowhere to Dennis' ears. Desperately he strained to locate the source, but huge waves blocked his view in every direction. Loud screeches and crashes added to his confusion, but now there was an undercurrent of sound that strangely resembled the chug of a diesel. A nearby geyser, following the usual shell scream, blinded him. Then, as he blinked his eyes to recover his sight, he saw through bleary eyes a craft that was almost upon him. It was an RAF patrol boat.

With motors almost idling and the crew apparently oblivious of the enemy fire which their little vessel had attracted, the boat eased up to Dennis. In the prow, pouring out directions to helmsman and crew in the fashion of a captain berthing a liner, stood an erect blue-clad figure.

As the launch carefully approached the bobbing flyer, Dennis fixed his eyes on the officer. He saw a gnarled, weather-worn face, etched with the lines of scores of sea years. And even in the excitement of the moment he found in the bearing of the old man a symbol of the pride and strength of Britain's seafarers. The biting voice that came to his ears, though cracked with age, sparkled with vigor and authority.

"Can ye make it, Laddie, if we put over the ladder?" he bellowed at Dennis.

"Ri . . . argh . . ." The sea washed the answer out of the youth's mouth.

But he was understood in spite of the impolite waves and two crewmen carefully hooked a resplendent chromium ladder to the gunwales. Needing no urging, Dennis let go his hold of the parachute lines at the same instant that he stretched out his arms to grab the tubular sidepieces. His hands seized the slippery metal and he heaved himself forward to lodge his foot on a lower rung. He felt his foot strike a crosspiece and for a second he rested. Then a vicious wave struck him, dashed him and the ladder against the side of the boat. There was a moment of doubt, then Dennis

sensed rather than felt the ladder detach itself from the launch. A second later it was sliding through his unsure grip. Still glittering in the rays of the sun as long as an inch remained above surface, it soon disappeared beneath the Channel waters. Dennis flopped back into the waves.

As the old captain saw what had happened, he emitted a groan. A stormy look came over his face. Hands on hips, he glared down at the floundering youth as the current carried him away from the boat. There was silence for a moment, then his angry voice roared across the waves.

"Here now! What d'ye think ye're doin'?"

"I'm . . . argh . . . argh." Dennis' reply was smothered by the sea.

"What ha' ye done wi' me ladder?"

Showering spray over captain, crew, and the half-drowned airman, a nearby shell-burst blotted out the reply that Dennis struggled to make.

"Forty years I've bin at sea and never seen such a bloomin' idjut," thundered the old man accusingly. "D'ye ha' no heart, ye blighter . . . the only chrumium ladder in the hull bloody Navy . . . ongrateful puppy ye throw it away . . . no more sense nor a Shanghai stevedore, ye . . ."

Only portions of the tirade carried to Dennis' ears as the craft circled about him, but they left no doubt in his mind of the captain's meaning. He swallowed great mouthfuls of the sea, while wondering if the old man was ever going to fish him out of the Channel. Far from being a symbol of all that was fine in British naval tradition, the captain, Dennis concluded, was a raving maniac. And as the harangue continued and the German batteries maintained their fire, the conviction grew in his mind that the old fool was quite willing to let him perish.

He looked around for the parachute. For some reason it had not collapsed and was still afloat. He decided to strike out for it and gain the added support it would afford him. Then he would let the old pirate talk till he was blue in the face, for he would be much better off than with only the Mae West to buoy him up.

He had taken but a few futile strokes when he felt strong arms grasping and hauling him aboard the rescue boat. Surprised that the vessel had slipped up behind him, Dennis stiffened at first, then sagged to permit himself to be poured onto the deck.

The blankets that were piled upon him, the hot drink that burned his throat, the delicious easiness that flooded him, drained his mind of all thought. It was not until almost a quarter of an hour had passed that he was even conscious of the steady chugging of the motor. Then with the awareness of engine noises there also came the realization that someone was talking to him. He opened one eye to squint at the speaker; then he quickly closed it again. The captain was still upbraiding him.

Accusations of ingratitude, waste, sabotage, and

several other varieties of crime were leveled at him.
He was told that he was not worth saving, and certainly not worth the loss of the only chromium ladder
in the entire Royal Navy. If he were any good at all,
he was informed, he would not have been shot down
by a Bosche in the first place.

"I'm sorry I lost your ladder. . . . I . . . I was a little
tired. . . ." he managed to blurt out weakly as he
interrupted the captain.

"Tired! Ye bloody well know ye were careless! If
ye'd had any sense, ye'd have held on to me ladder.
Mind ye, the only chrummium ladder in the hull . . ."
The old man seemed to find new energy and began his
verbal barrage anew.

Dennis tried to shut his ears to the tirade but to no
avail. At length, when his accusor paused for breath,
he decided to employ new tactics.

"Where," he asked diffidently, "is my parachute?"

". . . an if ye'd have had any . . . Did you say something?" asked the captain with a new note in his voice.

"Where is my chute?" repeated Dennis, but this
time with more confidence.

"An how would I know what ye've done with your
chute?" asked the old man.

"You mean you didn't fish it out?" said Dennis,
pressing what he detected as a note of doubt in the
other's voice.

"Ye had it last, and 'twas yer own responsibility,"
replied the captain defensively.

"I held it as long as *I* could," said Dennis, "and it was up to you to pick it up when I let go of it."

"Ye let go of it yerself," doggedly stated the old man, but without quite as much assurance as before.

"Well," asserted Dennis righteously, "I did *my* duty, anyway. But with the silk shortage and the orders on salvaging parachutes, the authorities may not accept your excuses. If you . . ."

"Excuses!" roared the captain. "Duty! No man ever accused John Simpson of failing to do his duty! I'll show ye, ye young puppy!"

Stomping away with all the dignity he could muster, the old sailor began bellowing orders. Sensing that something was afoot, Dennis pondered for a moment, and finally raised himself on his elbows to see what was taking place. He saw the captain, feet spread wide apart and standing immovable in the prow, scanning the sea through an antique telescope.

A vague feeling of uneasiness stole over Dennis as he watched and he asked himself what was up. He listened to the orders barked at the helmsman but could gather no clue of what was happening. Finally, he shook off the blankets in which he had been wrapped, and eased forward. He peered over the gunwales, but could see nothing but huge waves. Suddenly he heard a familiar shrieking noise and saw a nearby waterspout. That told him all he needed to know; incredible though it seemed, the captain had turned the little vessel about and brought it back to the vicinity in which Dennis had been rescued. And now he was searching for the lost parachute.

The reappearance of the patrol boat had inspired the Nazi artillerists to new heights. The drumfire of shells now became dangerously accurate and intense. Time and again the little vessel heeled over and rocked from close explosions. A dozen times over, Dennis closed his eyes in expectation of the blast that would blow them out of the sea. And through it all the old captain stood firm, bawling out orders for changes in course and speed.

Hours later, it seemed, the launch slowed down to almost a stop. Dennis looked up to find a crewman with a boathook and the glaring, muttering captain standing by. Then he peered over the side. A few feet away, still inflated but now bobbing as if anchored to the channel bottom, he saw his parachute. A moment later he was on his feet lending a hand to the sailor who had hooked the shrouds. Hand over hand they pulled in the silk. Then as the chute billowed over the small deck, Dennis leaned overboard to gather in the last few feet of the lines. It took more effort than he had supposed and, as he reeled in the wet cords, he idly wondered at the cause. Finally he estimated that there could be only inches more under water, and he gave a final tug. As he did so, hooked to the webbing of the harness, a bright, shiny, chromium ladder broke surface.

"Me ladder!"

The glad cry of the captain startled Dennis almost as much as the sight of the ladder, itself. For a precarious moment, as he balanced himself across the gunwales, his own fate and that of the prize ladder were in doubt. But Captain Simpson moved swiftly, and as he brushed Dennis to the deck, he gathered the chromium ladder to his arms.

"The only chrummium ladder in the hull blinkin' Navy!" he said admiringly. And, fondling it as if it were frail and precious, he carefully wiped it dry and placed it gently on the deck. He stared at it for a minute, lost in thought, then turned to Dennis.

" 'Tis a wonderful, wonderful thing, eh lad," he said quietly.

"The ladder, you mean, sir? Oh, quite," replied Dennis.

"The ladder?" said the captain with a touch of his former fire, "Ha' ye no sense? I mean yon parachute."

Dennis nodded his head in silent agreement.

# WORTH FIGHTING FOR
## by Hugh B. Cave

The jungle mist had spread a grim, gray shroud over the beach when Eddie Smith crept from his cot that morning. It was half an hour past dawn by his watch, but there was no dawn.

Rain had fallen through the night, drumming on the roof of the native shack in which he and eight others of the Base Force slept. Now the huts and tents of the PT base, the maintenance shops and pier installations were but ghostly shapes in a wet world.

Nothing in that strange, war-created world seemed alive as Eddie went past the squadron office and the radio shack, and stopped a little distance from the pier, anxiously searching the mist for the incoming boats.

It was not a new thing, this morning vigil. He had

done it day after day, for weeks. It was a kind of torture that he almost enjoyed, this business of watching the boats come in from their nightly patrols.

Because he, Eddie Smith, radioman second class assigned to the Base Force, wanted nothing on earth more than to ride one of those sleek slivers of plywood.

Lieutenant Bradley's boat was the first one in this morning. He watched it nose up to the pier, a slim gray ghost in the mist, and heard the crew talking as they made the craft fast. He heard one of the men say with weary vehemence, "We got that Jap, Skipper. He never made it back to base, burning the way he was. We won't get credit for it, but there's one less destroyer on Tojo's books this morning!"

"Seems as though we never get credit for what we do on these night patrols," another voice said. The speaker was not grousing, he was simply stating a fact.

Eddie waited until the last boat was in before he crept back to the shack. The mist was lifting by then. From the shack doorway he could look out over the sea—that deceptively peaceful sea—and make out the lumpy, greenish shapes of nearby islands.

The South Sea Islands! Think of it—an eighteen-year-old kid from number 9 Elm Street, Brookdale, Connecticut, spending four months on a coral atoll whose inhabitants, until a little while ago, had never laid eyes on a white man!

There was only one thing wrong with it. Home was

too far away. The kid from Brookdale, Connecticut, was homesick.

It was midafternoon when Eddie entered the squadron office. He wanted to see Lieutenant Commander Roberts, the squadron Commanding Officr who had been out on the night patrol and had slept most of the morning. Commander Roberts was talking in low tones to Lieutenant Bradley when Eddie entered.

The Squadron Commander looked up at last, and Eddie timidly approached. "Sir," he said, "I try not to be a pest, but——" His grin was sheepish. He was not afraid of Commander Roberts. The Commander was old, around thirty-five, but seemed to know what went on inside a fellow.

Commander Roberts turned to Lieutenant Bradley and said, smiling, "Smith wants to ride one of the boats."

Lieutenant Bradley looked tired. He was not much more than a kid himself, twenty-three, and he, too, had been out all night on patrol. Moreover, his boat had been in a battle. He said, "Yes, I know," and scowled at Eddie. In his next remark there was more than a touch of cynicism.

"Just why do you want to ride the boats, Smith?"

Eddie felt uncomfortable under the stare, and hesitated. He knew why he wanted to ride the boats, and it was really simple. But how would it sound if he said to the Lieutenant, "I'm homesick. I go crazy tied down at the base here all the time. I want to get

out there and help lick those Japs, so we can get the
war over with and—go home."

*And go home.* It wouldn't sound good at all. It
would sound shaky and scared! The lieutenant would
never understand.

It was characteristic of Eddie Smith that, shunning
one extreme, he went to the other. "I want to do my
bit, sir," he said slowly, aware that he had said the
same thing before, often, and was only repeating himself. "I—I figure freedom and democracy are worth
fighting for, and I want to do my duty."

Even that didn't sound just right after he had said
it. Not at all as convincing as when, at home, he had
heard silver-tongued radio orators delivering the same
sort of speech. He wondered uneasily if the radio
orators would sound as convincing if they were suddenly transplanted to some sticky, insect-ridden island
in the South Pacific, and he didn't blame Lieutenant
Bradley for sneering.

"Very noble," the Lieutenant said, unable to hide
the weariness in his voice. "Very patriotic, Smith. But
the boats are in good hands." He shrugged his
shoulders. "Is there anything else you wanted?"

Eddie Smith felt that thickening in his throat again.
"N—no, sir," he said, and went out.

It was the next afternoon when Eddie began to
think that something was wrong with him. He was
on duty in the radio shack, and it was hot, sticky hot.
When Hyde, the chief radioman, came in, Eddie

leaned back with a groan and said, "Boy, what I could do to a nice tall glass of lemonade! This must be the hottest day we've had."

Hyde, a dour, thin man who had served in the Navy a long time, gave him a queer look. "Is it?" he said. "The thermometer says it's the coolest day this month." He came closer and looked carefully into Eddie's eyes, because you could sometimes tell a lot by the whites of a man's eyes. He couldn't be sure of Eddie's until he stared into them.

"You're sick, kid," Hyde said. "Better go lie down."

Next morning Eddie was not at the pier when the night patrol came in. He didn't see the string of jagged holes made by a Jap twenty-millimeter gun under the plexiglass of Lieutenant Bradley's boat, nor hear the slow tread of the men who carried Bradley's radioman, Earl Andrews, ashore on a stretcher. Eddie wasn't there. He was in bed with a temperature. Malaria, dengue fever, he wasn't sure what he had, but it was getting worse by the hour. He hadn't slept all night, and in a little while he would have to quit kidding himself and report sick.

About ten o'clock one of the men came in and told him about Earl Andrews. "Hit in both legs," the man said, "when a Jap 'can' opened up on them at close range in the dark. The Doc patched him up and they're sending him out by plane, to a hospital."

Then and there Eddie decided that he was not sick. Not sick at all. He got out of bed. He put on his

Marine-issue shoes and dungarees, splashed cold water
on his face until the flush was gone, and stuffed a hand-
ful of pills into his pocket. He went down to the radio
shack and was there, hard at work, when Commander
Roberts came in an hour later.

The Commander had no time for pleasantries that
morning. He was all Navy, and grim. A PT squadron
of eight boats and eighty men and a small base force is
a close-knit unit, and Commander Roberts looked
upon each of his men as a comrade. When one of them
was hurt, when the Japs brought pain and suffering to
some member of that compact little group, Roberts
suffered, too.

"Smith," he said without preamble, "you're getting
what you asked for. From now on you'll ride with
Lieutenant Bradley."

Eddie could only say, "Y–yes, sir."

At the door the Commander paused for an instant.
"I'd go light on the oratory," he said gently, "if I were
you. The Lieutenant's brother was on Bataan."

"I'll keep my mouth shut, sir," Eddie replied
humbly.

He remembered the commander's words when he
reported for duty that night, and it helped to steady
him when he faced the lieutenant. It helped, somehow, to soften the glint in Bradley's eyes.

"Remember this," Bradley said bluntly. "There are
ten men on a PT boat, and every one of them has to
do his job, his whole job, every minute we're out

there. The life of every man on board depends on
that."

"Yes, sir."

"You're to maintain radio contact with the other
three boats all the time we're on patrol." His scowl
thinned a little. "What's the matter? Don't you feel
well?"

Eddie replied quickly that he had never felt better
in his life, he was just excited at being assigned to a
boat.

The moon was strange and bleak, misty even when
the scudding clouds parted to let it shine undimmed.
Or was that an illusion, created by his fever? He sat
by the radio, aware of every vibrant throb of the three
powerful engines as the PT, second to leave the pier,
swung through the wake of Commander Roberts' boat
ahead.

Night patrol! He knew what that meant. Hour
after endless hour, these four midget thunderboats
would prowl the sea, on guard against any move by the
enemy to put troops ashore on American-held islands
in the region.

If the enemy did try, there would be a brief, savage
skirmish in the dark, victory for one side, defeat for
the other. More often than not it was the Japs who
fled home disorganized, but there had been times, and
would be again, when a PT boat failed to return to
base. You never knew.

He had nothing much to do at first. The patrols

were well established; each boat knew its assignment
and there was no need for commands.

An hour had passed. Two. The moon still cast that
ghostly glow, silvering the water and the boat's wake,
but the other PT's were no longer in sight, and Eddie
realized vaguely that he and the nine other men
aboard this one were on their own. The blurred
shape of an island, Arundel, perhaps, or Kolomban-
gara, swelled to port.

It was after midnight when Burke, the torpedo-man,
paused at his elbow. "Better keep your tin hat handy,
kid," he said. But Eddie did not answer. Fiddling with
the radio he had stumbled on a voice that jerked him
to attention—a sharp, jabbering voice which spoke not
English but Japanese!

He was still tense until Burke said with a shrug,
"Just a radioman on some Jap ship, kid. None of our
concern unless he happens to be in our bailiwick."

But suddenly Burke was tense, too. In the cockpit
Lieutenant Bradley was shouting the call to General
Quarters!

Eddie had never dreamed it would be like this. Back
at the base he had often heard the PT men talk: "Ran
into three of 'em tonight, three destroyers," or "There
we were, see?—cruisin' along at slow speed when all of
a sudden this Jap loomed up dead ahead!" Eddie had
taken their talk at face value. Now he realized how
pitifully inadequate the English language really was!

Or was it? Because later, he himself would probably

say of the awesome, onrushing shapes in the eerie moonlight ahead: "There we were, see?—and all at once these four Japs were almost on top of us."

Four Japs. They had not seen the PT boat yet and were pulling along in line, a cruiser and three destroyers. Eddie's heart beat faster at sight of them; his fingertips quivered and he thought vaguely, "Im scared. Gee, I'm scared!" But it was all right to be scared that way. Sure it was. There was no panic mixed up in it.

Then he realized that he had been standing like a statue, staring. And Lieutenant Bradley was yelling at him.

"You, Smith! Get on the job! Send out their position. Tell the Commander we're going to attack!"

Eddie moved then. The flush that swept his face was not a fever flush; it was born of the realization that Lieutenant Bradley thought he was too frightened to move. There had been impatience and a kind of derision in the Lieutenant's clipped voice; derision for a man who, after blabbing nobly about fighting for freedom and democracy, had tightened up and gone into a trance at sight of danger. Only he *hadn't* done that! The sight of those big ships had awed him; that was all.

As he carried out the skipper's orders, Eddie felt a change in the rhythm of the engines, a slackening of the PT's speed. Bradley had changed course and slowed the boat to a crawl, so that the Japs on those four huge warships would not spot her wake. Barely crawling now, the marauding PT swung into position for a torpedo shot.

Stillson, the quartermaster, was conning the boat on target, talking in a low, sure voice that betrayed no tension. "They're doing about thirty knots, Skipper, I think. That big one's a cruiser, Mogami class. Eight-inch guns. Steady now—a little left—hold her steady."

No one else was talking. It was as though the little thunderboat were a thing alive, holding its breath while crouching for a sudden savage leap. Actually that feeling of suspended motion was an illusion; the PT rolled crazily in the sea, and the three powerful engines below deck still purred out sufficient speed to give her headway. But you felt, all the same, that a heart had momentarily stopped beating and time was standing still.

Suddenly the quartermaster's voice broke the spell. "Now, sir, now!"

There was a sharp, shrill, rushing sound, a hiss of air under pressure, as the after torpedo tubes loosed their deadly fish. The Jap was not an easy target—at thirty knots no target is easy—but he was in range, nicely in range, and unsuspecting. Every man aboard the marauding boat held his breath. The quarter-master's hand rose and fell, tolling off the seconds.

"Missed him," Lieutenant Bradley said bitterly.

But the Jap had seen the white wakes of those two torpedoes, and now he erred. His bow swung wide; he

was a broadside target big as a barn. Flame belched
from his turrets as his big guns roared a challenge.
Wildly his searchlights tunneled the dark.

Stillson's voice was a scream of elation. "Hit him,
skipper! Hit him!"

The two forward torpedoes hissed as the impulse
charges jabbed them to action. And then some grinning god of ill luck took a hand. Aboard the PT boat,
pandemonium broke loose.

One of the two fish, slipping from its tube, had
stuck fast!

Eddie Smith instinctively ducked as the shower of
sparks from the jammed torpedo rained over the deck.
His foot struck the engine room hatch and he fell
sprawling, picked himself up and clung to a turret to
steady himself. In the glare of the fireworks display
he could see the faces of his boatmates, bleak and
grim. In a heartbeat of time they had grown older.
They were doing their jobs, though. The turret-guns
chattered viciously. The heavier, noisier oerlikon
thundered a sullen reply to the Jap's fire. What was it
Lieutenant Bradley had said? "There are ten men on
a PT boat, and every one of them has to do his job,
his whole job, every minute!"

Bradley was doing *his* job now, at the wheel, but
his voice, shouting orders, was lost in the ragged chatter
of the stuck torpedo. Ensign Frank Rand, stumbling
toward the torpedo tube, had fallen over the crumpled
form of Burke, the torpedoman, and lay writhing, he

and Burke both cut down by the murderous twenty-millimeter fire from the cruiser.

And the stuck torpedo was working. Its propeller, spinning, beat a shrill clatter against the walls of the tube. Out of water with nothing to cool it, wobbling crazily as it hissed and sputtered, the fish was glowing now, getting hot.

Eddie knew vaguely what that meant. A "hot run" was not always dangerous, but in a sea such as this, the fish might cock itself. Then a pounding wave could slap its nose and blow the boat and everyone on her to bits!

He acted instinctively, but how he kept his feet as the craft beneath him leaped wildly through a flying turn, he never knew. He saw Lieutenant Bradley at the wheel, twisting and turning the boat to dodge the Jap's fire. He stumbled over Ensign Rand and got up again. The silvery shaft of a Jap searchlight stabbed through the dark above the sea and singled him out, fastened on him, and he struggled through its blinding glare like a moth wriggling on a pin.

Snatching Burke's mallet, he swung it with all his might. That was the thing to do—fire the jammed torpedo by percussion! Get it out of there! But the effort of stumbling to the tube, through the Jap's fire, had brought back with a rush all the fever and sickness which had been bottled up inside him, and he had to swing the mallet again and again, blindly, until at last he hit what he was aiming at.

He fell to his knees then as the torpedo shot from the tube. He saw it splash into the sea, and realized dazedly that if it ran true to course it would hit something because the cruiser had cut across the PT's bow and was in the way of it.

He didn't care, really. Too sick to watch, he collapsed on deck as the PT hiked her nose out of the heaving sea and lit for home with the three metal monsters under her deck roaring their total thunder. Weaving, twisting, with Lieutenant Bradley at the wheel and smoke pouring out astern, the little boat had put peril behind her.

The explosion seemed a long way off. A very long way off, Eddie was disappointed. He had expected a bigger sound, something cataclysmic. Or perhaps the sound had been loud, but he was too sick to know it.

When he turned his head wearily to look back at the enemy force, he saw a raging tower of flame reaching to the sky, and Jap destroyers circling helplessly about the edge of it.

"That's good," he thought. "We hit a cruiser. The war's that much nearer won." And then his musings were no longer coherent. He had no control over them.

He lay in a heap on the deck, sick with fever, and thought of home, of the white, blue-shuttered cottage at number 9 Elm Street. He saw himself strolling up the street on a summer evening, waving to Sally Edwards on her porch, stopping to talk with Tommy

Whelan, the cop. He thought of his mother and her
apple pies, and his kid brother, Jimmy, crawling under
the piano in the rumpus room, after table-tennis balls.
He thought of his dad, holding forth to Mr. Brooks,
next door, on politics and taxes . . . and of the garage
window he'd promised to fix but hadn't . . . and . . .

"I want to go home," he thought dully. "That's all
that matters. I want to get the war over with and go
home."

Then he opened his eyes and looked up into the
scowling face of Lieutenant Bradley, who was bending
over him. And Eddie realized that he had spoken that
last thought out loud, and Lieutenant Bradley had
heard it.

The boat was speeding through the night, back to
base, and the Lieutenant just stood there glaring.
Eddie's sickness was not physical then; it was a hollow,
empty feeling that swelled inside him and made him
want to die. He saw the Lieutenant motion to two of
the men, and they picked Eddie up and carried him
below and left him there. They didn't say a word.

It was the end of everything. Eddie knew that. He
would never again ride Lieutenant Bradley's boat.
Sick with shame, he shut his eyes.

Then, as from a distance, he heard Lieutenant
Bradley's voice. The Skipper had come alone into the
crew's quarters and was quietly standing there beside
Eddie's bunk.

"Are you all right?" he was saying.

"I—I guess so, sir," Eddie managed.

The lieutenant sat down and looked at him for a minute or two. Just looked. And then he said, "You did a good job, Smith. I was wrong about you."

"Wrong?" Eddie whispered.

"I thought you'd been sounding off with all that fancy talk to cover up the fact that—well, I thought it was just talk, Smith." The Lieutenant hesitated, seemingly at a loss for exactly the right words. But then he leaned forward. He was still frowning, but his eyes and voice were soft now, and warm.

"We don't need big words out here to explain what we're fighting for, kid," he said then, gently. "That sort of stuff is all right for the folks back home—maybe they need the orators to stir them up—but out here we know why we're fighting and we're not ashamed of it. We all want to go home, Eddie. Every man in the squadron is so homesick right now that he could crawl into a hole and bawl his eyes out."

He stood up, and he was once again Lieutenant Bradley, skipper of a PT boat, a man with a job to do and no time to waste. But he had one more thing to say, and he said it.

"That's what we're fighting for," he declared softly. "Something to go home to. And tonight, kid, thanks to you, we're a step nearer our destination."

# THE
# LOST COMPANY
## by William Chamberlain

The company—what there was left of it—limped back
to the shelter of the woods behind the crest of the little
hill where it had bivouacked the night before. Tanks
clattered and growled and slid in the fresh snow as the
night came down; tired men, who had been fighting
for five days now, peered through the hovering fog
with bleared eyes and knew that this was not good.

They had been cut off when the Germans had
smashed at St. Vith. Now they were on their own—
their supply trains God knew where, and with the gas
running low in their gas tanks and their ammunition
nearly gone.

No, not good.

Capt. Eddie Mulhouse, who had come to command

the company a scant week before the Germans had started their drive through the Ardennes, climbed stiffly out of his tank and beat his hands together to warm them. There was a farmhouse here in the hollow behind the hill, its occupants gone now as the Germans came again. He had stayed here last night, and now he made his way back into the deserted kitchen, lighted the candle, which was still thrust into the neck of a wine bottle on the table, and stood looking at the disorder which the people who had once lived here had left.

A child's smock, torn and soiled, on the floor, and a rocking chair overturned and with one rocker broken. The last of a loaf of dark bread beside the candle and a woman's shawl wadded in a corner. Somehow, the sight of those things angered Eddie Mulhouse a little. War could be so personal, he was thinking. It stripped people naked and laid all of their intimate little secrets bare to strangers who neither knew nor cared.

He shrugged the thought away as he spread his soiled map on the table; dropped to a stool to study it with his lean face twisted into a scowl. He'd send for his platoon leaders presently, and Sergeant Hoeffer should be getting back from his scout to the east. Then they'd know better where they stood. Maybe they would.

Eddie Mulhouse was twenty-nine and slight, and with clipped sandy hair above his homely, serious face. Back home he had owned a service station before the

Army had tapped him for a grimmer kind of service.

Responsibility sat heavily on his shoulders now; responsibility for the hundred and seventeen men who were left to him and who were looking to him—a little doubtfully, he knew—for the answer to this mess.

That doubt was unspoken, but he had been able to feel it ever since he had taken command of the company. He was aware of the question mark in men's eyes who watched a commander who was a stranger to them and who was as yet unproved. And St. Vith had done nothing to wash away those question marks, because St. Vith had been a howling confusion of Germans driving in out of the fog and, when the thing was done, the outfit had been reeling back and the company had been cut off and left behind. So now they had returned to this low hill with its firs standing like gloomy sentinels in the last of the day, and to the drear farmhouse which hunkered like an old man in the snow with its empty windows peering like sad eyes into the murk.

Feet scraped outside and Sergeant Hoeffer came in then, a stolid man with a dirty scarf wrapped around his neck. He stamped the snow from his feet and blinked in the candlelight.

"We got as far as Verguelles, sir," he said heavily. "Germans there—lots of 'em. So we tried to cut south. Germans there too. Damn it, the whole country is full of the buzzards!"

Eddie Mulhouse nodded absently. "I guess we're

cut off, sergeant," he said. "Not so good."

"Pretty bad," Hoeffer agreed. "What do we do now?"

"Tell the platoon commanders that I want to see them," Eddie Mulhouse said tiredly.

"Second platoon's still back by the crossroads," Hoeffer said. "That's Carr's platoon—shall I tell 'em to come in?"

"Tell them to come in," Mulhouse answered him. "With the Germans all around us, an outpost back there's no good."

"Useless as a fifth leg on a dog," Sergeant Hoeffer grunted sourly. "I'll tell 'em."

Back at the crossroads three tanks huddled in the shelter of a fir clump. "Come tomorrow and we'll be measuring the gas we got left with an eye-dropper, if we don't catch up to the trains pretty soon," the man said, straightening angrily.

His name was Jason Carr and he was a sergeant, commanding the platoon now. A slender, whipcorded man with a seamed face and the lean legs of a cavalry-man, for he had worn the Army's cloth back in the days before they had taken the horses away and had given the cavalry stinking machines instead. That change had not pleased him. Other things pleased him even less right now—things like the German tanks which had come lumbering through the Ardennes in the December fog, and things like storm troopers, dressed in stolen GI uniforms, who lurked in the dark patches of woods which dotted the broken hills.

And the thing that pleased Jason Carr the least of all was Capt. Eddie Mulhouse, who had come to command the company a scant ten days ago and who had been crawling around in rompers when he had first thrown a leg over a McClellan saddle. The grapevine had it that Eddie Mulhouse used to run a garage or service station or something like that before the war— and that was no way to learn to command a cavalry outfit, in Jason Carr's book, even if the cavalry rode tanks now instead of horses.

Private Simmons, bow gunner of Tank 2, leaned his back against the tank's cold hull. He was twenty, and had a way with a machine gun.

"Come tomorrow and maybe we're dead," he said cheerfully, in answer to Jason Carr. "What you want to borrow trouble for, Sarge? A man would think that you don't like this country."

"I don't," Carr said roughly. "And I don't have to borrow trouble. I got all the trouble I need."

"Come on, now!" Private Simmons said. "A young sprig like you! How was it with Custer, Jase?"

"I don't go back that far," Carr said sourly.

It wasn't that he disliked the captain, he was thinking. It was just that Eddie Mulhouse was too new to the company, and the bars were too shiny on his collar. In the old Army a man could go for fifteen years before he was good enough to command a troop. He didn't peddle gas one day and command a company the next.

Private First Class Moody poked his head through the hatch. "Orders is to close up with the rest of the company where we bivouacked last night, Sarge," he said thinly. "Up by that farmhouse."

Carr nodded; he hauled himself up to the hatch and swung his arm. Saw the gesture repeated from the other tanks down the short column. Only two others now— the rest had been knocked out day before yesterday. Beneath him, the engine growled into life and the big machine lurched forward, stinking of hot oil and clattering with the noisy racket which always angered Carr a little.

He pulled gloves onto his stiff fingers and stared ahead into the dying afternoon while resentment grew in him. Not like the old days, he thought bitterly, when he had ridden with a real cavalry outfit. Ridden with the horsehead insigne, black against its background of yellow, on his shoulder, and his rifle slung in its boot beneath his knee. Not hunched in the narrow turret of a stinking tank, like a fat woman squeezed into a taxi. Or like a grease monkey in a garage service car!

Tank 2 nosed through a notch in the hills, the other tanks following, and dipped down into a shallow draw where the farmhouse stood at the edge of the trees. Other tanks dotted the snow down there. The platoon went on and presently a soldier waved them off the road and toward the shelter of the trees, and then came on to Tank 2 as it clanked to a halt.

"Gas up," he said—it was MacCauley, bugler and messenger, Carr saw. "Rear echelon, what we got left of it, is over there to the right. Then report to Captain Mulhouse at the Command Post."

Private Simmons pushed up beside Carr. "Hi, Bus," he called down. "What's the good word?"

"I ain't heard," MacCauley said, grinning through the murk. "I guess we're moving out again."

"Where to?" Simmons wanted to know.

"Paris," MacCauley told him. "Where did you think? They're puttin' on a special show for us tonight at the Folies Berrygare. Or didn't you know?"

"I don't get around much any more," Private Simmons answered. "Save me a seat if I'm late."

The platoon leaders filed into the kitchen of the farmhouse, Jason Carr coming last. There was Art Persons—pudgy and usually good-humored, but with deep lines around his mouth now and his smile gone—and Fred Dickey, who had gone to Princeton, and Jethro Hunter, a spare and silent man from Vermont. And Jason Carr.

Eddie Mulhouse looked at them for a moment while he thought of the things that he wanted to say. And yet there wasn't much that a man really could say, was there? Nothing much that they didn't already know. And this was no time for one of those pep talks that you read about.

So he said finally, "Sergeant Hoeffer got back a

little while ago. He says that we're cut off from the east and south. We've already tried the other directions. You know what happened."

They didn't say anything: just stood there looking at him, and again Eddie Mulhouse could feel the pressure of the questioning in their eyes. They were looking to him for the answer to this—and there was nobody to whom he could turn for an answer. Nobody at all. Just Eddie Mulhouse, the service-station grease monkey! Well, he might as well give them the whole dose right now.

"We've got no radio contact," he said, whipping his words at them. "We're nearly out of gas and almost as bad off for ammunition. The krauts may hit us tonight. They will hit us tomorrow for sure. Anybody got any ideas?"

He saw the uncertainty wash across the faces of the officers as they avoided his stare. Then Sergeant Carr's face seemed to stand out. Anger was creasing it, deepening the little gullies about the older man's mouth.

"I say let's get out of here!" Carr said violently.

Eddie Mulhouse studied him with narrowed eyes. He had not been in the company long enough to know Sgt. Jason Carr very well. Knew him only as a cantankerous man who was a regular and who had brought with him into the outfit all of the prejudices and the dislikes of the old Army.

"Get out where, sergeant?" Eddie Mulhouse asked tightly.

The angry spark deepened in Carr's eyes. "Anywhere," he said. "That's better than sitting here waiting to be gobbled up like a bunch of geese!"

Eddie Mulhouse didn't answer that right away. For a moment his mind wandered back to the well-remembered details of his service station at home—the pumps standing there at attention, their hoses neatly looped up and waiting to pour their life fluid into the thousands of cars which streamed through the bustling city. Those pumps were trying to tell something, Eddie Mulhouse thought vaguely.

He had it, then, and it was the answer to Jason Carr's angry comment.

"We've got enough gas left for maybe two hours of operating," he said, his voice flattening out with certainty now. "We can't afford to spend that gas running around in circles without knowing where we're going. And we don't know that now—so we stay here."

He saw the faint shock that spread over the faces of the men in front of him. Jason Carr gestured angrily. "Cavalry's supposed to move, Captain," he said, and the eyes of the other platoon leaders turned to look at him as he spoke. "It wasn't meant to squat on a hill someplace like an old hen! Even tank cavalry!"

He had to take hold of this thing, Eddie Mulhouse thought. Nobody else was going to do it for him. That was what a man bargained for when he accepted the bars on his collar.

"We'll set up a perimeter here," he said. There was

a new crispness in his voice. "Dig the tanks in and camouflage them. Divide up the ammunition and gas. We'll hold here until help comes."

Sgt. Jason Carr shuffled forward a little, his face grim. This was all wrong, he was thinking. It was what came of putting a grease monkey in command of cavalry.

"Sir," he said, his voice hoarse, "about seventy years ago a cavalry outfit died on a hill above the Little Big Horn because it sat there and waited for help to come to it! This outfit can die the same way if we stay here!"

This thing was getting out of hand, Eddie Mulhouse knew. He'd have to chop it down with a sharp blade. His thoughts were clear now. He was right—he knew that he was right. You didn't run tanks without gas. Everything must be put aside except that single consideration. To start out from here now would mean that dawn would find them stranded, with the precious fuel gone; nothing left then for them but to wait for the end. That was the way it would be.

"We still form a perimeter!" Eddie Mulhouse said, his voice whipping out at them.

For a moment, Sergeant Carr stood there looking back. Then he said, his face darkening, "Commanding Cavalry is different from running a service station, Captain."

"Is it?" Eddie Mulhouse asked softly. Then his voice hardened again. "You have my orders, gentlemen. Move out!"

Sgt. Jason Carr stared for a moment longer; then long habit stiffened his shoulders and dropped an impassive mask across his leathery face. He said, "Yes, sir," and his words were echoed by the other men.

They went, then, shuffling their feet across the snow at the threshold of the kitchen's door. Only Sergeant Hoeffer remained, shadowy in the candlelight at the back of the room. Eddie Mulhouse swung around on him; wondered if he, too, felt that this was a trap that he was putting the company into.

"Well?" he demanded, his voice more harsh than he had intended.

Sergeant Hoeffer rubbed a heavy hand across the stubble on his chin. "Don't let Jase Carr ride you, sir," he said finally. "He's old Army and things new bother him. Even officers. But he's a good man. You can count on him when the chips are down."

Art Persons, walking with Jethro Hunter back through the snow, put into words the things that both were thinking. "We going to get out of this, Jethro?"

"No," Jethro said in his flat, nasal voice. "I don't think so. I wish I was back home in Vermont."

Over in the second platoon, Private Simmons was thinking the same thing. Only he was wishing that he was back in Yonkers. He said that to Private First Class Moody as the two of them squatted with their backs against Tank 2 and waited for Jason Carr to come back and tell them what to do.

"You hadn't ought to talk that way," Moody said.

"The way I see it, we're needed up here or we wouldn't be here. The Army knows what it's doing, I guess."

"Since when?" Private Simmons asked skeptically. "Me, I think it's just another foul-up."

Moody's face was faintly shocked. "I don't think that you should say that either," he said angrily.

"I'm exercising my rights," Simmons told him loftily. "I'm making with my free speech. Ain't that what we're fighting for?"

"I guess so," Moody answered in a dubious voice.

Sgt. Jason Carr came then. "Load up," he said in a brittle voice. "We'll move a couple of hundred yards to the west and go into position there."

"Go into position to do what, Sarge?" Private Simmons wanted to know, getting to his feet.

Jason Carr gave him a flinty glance. "To die, maybe," he said. "You got any objections?"

Eddie Mulhouse made a round of the perimeter at midnight; everything had been quiet so far, but he felt in his bones that that wouldn't last. They must, he felt sure, be ahead of the American lines which had gone reeling back at St. Vith. Presently the Germans would come along the two roads which crossed here in the little valley below the abandoned farmhouse.

Fog made gray wraiths in the hooded glow of his flashlight as he came to where the second platoon was lying, its three tanks partly dug into the frozen ground. Sergeant Carr was huddled in a foxhole, a blanket over his shoulders, as Eddie squatted beside him.

"Everything quiet, Sergeant?" Mulhouse asked.

Jason Carr rubbed his hand along his face. There was something new that had come into the captain's voice now, he thought uncertainly. Something which reminded him somehow of a man with whom he had used to ride, back in the days when he had worn the horsehead patch on his shoulder. The idea comforted him a little.

"Nothing moves except the wind," he answered and a little of the irritable rasp had gone out of his voice.

Eddie Mulhouse said, "Good. Maybe our luck will hold," and went on into the night, his shielded flashlight making a faint yellow tracery against the snow. . . .

Just before dawn, the third platoon, guarding the western approach, captured a prisoner. A surly, heavyset man dressed in a GI uniform. Jethro Hunter brought him into the kitchen CP, a pistol jammed into the small of the man's back.

"Caught him sneaking through the trees," Jethro said laconically. "He rings like a lead dollar to me, Eddie."

And the man finally talked as Sergeant Hoeffer stood over him, his face hard and remorseless. Eddie Mulhouse had been right. The company was surrounded and the knoll where it lay was important to those people out there, for it blocked the way to the west. The Germans would attack as soon as daylight came.

It was just short of 0800 hours and the snow had started to fall again when the first attack started. Tanks thrusting the snouts of their guns out of a dark patch of woods a mile away. They came on, waddling inexorably across the empty ground as Eddie Mulhouse waited and watched with the second platoon. They were less than three hundred yards away when he finally gave the word, for there was no ammunition to waste now.

Then he dropped a hand and the somber morning echoed with the snarl of gunfire. When the echoes had died away at last three of the German tanks were broken hulks and smoke boiled from another. The rest were moving back to the shelter of the woods.

Eddie Mulhouse said softly, "Nice shooting, Sergeant. But they'll come again."

Twice more during the morning they tried it, coming in from the south and west now. And twice more they went back licking their wounds. But not without a price. One of Jethro Hunter's tanks was gone now, most of its crew with it. The fourth platoon had six men down. They were holding, Eddie Mulhouse thought as he made the rounds again, but for how long? This couldn't last forever.

The shelling started then. Heavy stuff which crumped down on the knoll, knocking limbs off the dour firs and tossing up geysers of dirty snow. And it took its toll. A man here and a man there and the totals kept on mounting. Private First Class Moody was gone in the second platoon, and Mike Borden in the third, and Pete Porforio in the first. No more roll calls for them.

Eddie Mulhouse came back to the kitchen from an inspection of the perimeter in the afternoon and found Sergeant Hoeffer hunched over the radio in the corner. A faint excitement washed Hoeffer's square face as he turned his head.

"I got the Command Post of Combat Command B, Captain," he said hoarsely. "They want to talk to you."

Eddie Mulhouse took the head phones and a voice came faintly to him through the crackling static. "This is Colonel Stamford," it said. "Where are you, Mulhouse?"

"About two miles west of Verguelles, sir," Eddie said. "Dug in on a little knoll by a farmhouse. We're under heavy attack."

"How's your gas and ammunition?"

"Almost gone," Eddie said.

The voice in the head phones was silent for a moment. Then it said soberly, "You're holding up most of a German corps, Mulhouse. Can you hang on until tomorrow morning? I think that we can get help to you by then."

It was Eddie Mulhouse's turn to be silent for a moment. Then he said, no expression in his voice, "We'll hang on," and let his breath go out in a short sigh.

"It's important," the colonel told him urgently. "Good luck, boy."

Eddie Mulhouse took off the head phones and put them down gently, conscious that Sergeant Hoeffer was watching him with a face which had grown gray and old. Eddie forced his own mouth into a grin.

"They'll get help up to us tomorrow, Hoeffer," he said. "I think everything will be all right."

"Tomorrow," Sergeant Hoeffer answered, taking a long time with his words, "is a long time away, Captain."

Another tank attack came in just as the last of the day was dying. A big one this time, and for a long moment it looked as though it was going to go through. The last of the ammunition was going now and this couldn't last much longer. But the fury of fire from the knoll was enough once more, and presently the attacking wave rolled back, leaving its crippled hulks behind, and the company breathed again and settled into its holes once more.

The thing had not been bought cheaply, though. More men of the company down; more of its tanks silent now. And Art Persons came into the CP with his hands shaking and his eyes staring and blood streaking his face where a flying splinter of steel had raked him.

Sgt. Jason Carr brought him in, for all sense of time or place had left Art Persons and he had wandered over to where the second platoon lay. Now, he stood in front of the table where a new candle burned and lashed Eddie Mulhouse with his stare.

"How much do you think that flesh and blood can stand?" he yelled at Eddie. "We haven't got a chance, I tell you! Half of my platoon is dead! We've got to give up! We've got to send a flag out to them and——

Eddie Mulhouse shook his head tiredly. "We hang on, Art," he said. "We'll get help tomorrow."

Art Persons' crazy laughter filled the disordered kitchen. "Tomorrow we'll all be dead," he said thickly then. "Our gas is gone. Our ammunition is gone. What do we fight with now?"

"Our fists, I guess, if we have to," Eddie Mulhouse told him. "Lie down a while, Art. You'll feel better."

For a moment, Art Persons peered with bloodshot eyes; then wheeled abruptly and went across the room and lay, face down, on the tumbled cot that was there. Sergeant Carr stirred uneasily, half turning toward the door.

"Things are pretty bad, Captain," he said, but there was a grudging respect in his voice now.

Eddie Mulhouse nodded absently. "We'll make out, Sergeant," he said. "Tell your men that we're holding up the advance of a German corps. They'll like to know that."

On impulse, Sergeant Carr came to attention and saluted; then wheeled out into the growing dark again. He was feeling better about this. By heaven, that was the sort of talk that he used to hear from the officers back in his old outfit! It was good talk to hear!

The night passed, endless minute crawling after endless minute and the shells crumping down like the bongs of a giant bell which tolled solemnly for the dead. And then the gray dawn came finally and the company braced itself for the new attack which would come. It would be the last one, Eddie Mulhouse knew, for, after this one had come in, the company would have nothing left to shoot.

But there was that gas left in his gas tanks, he knew. That was his reserve—the few precious gallons which he had saved by digging in here on the hill. So they wouldn't wait in their holes this time for that attack; they'd go out to meet it instead. And they'd meet it where the Germans didn't expect that it would be met. That was the plan that he had made as the night had ticked on. The surprise would give them one more shot in their locker; perhaps be enough to buy the few more hours that they needed until help came.

He passed the word along and the tanks—those that were able—crawled back out of their holes. The gas from the disabled tanks was divided and crewmen replaced, and then the company waited again. Mid-morning passed and still the attack didn't come.

Private Simmons, squatting in the shelter of Tank 2, turned to Sgt. Jason Carr.

"What happens next, Jase?" he asked in the tone of a man who didn't much care.

"I don't know, kid," Jason Carr said.

"You think that Captain Mulhouse knows?" Simmons asked.

Jason Carr thought that over for a long minute. Then he nodded his head slowly. "Yeah," he said. "I think he does, kid. I guess he's a pretty good man." And that was high praise from Jason Carr.

The new attack came just before noon—grunting machines deployed across the open ground in front of the knoll and steaming remorselessly on. But the company wasn't on the knoll now. Eddie Mulhouse had moved it through the trees to the flank, where it lay hidden by the fog in a deep fold in the ground. And then Eddie Mulhouse blew his whistle so that it blasted clear and loud in the murky noon, and the company went in. Went in hard with eleven tanks racking forward and the last of the precious gas turning tracks which pawed eagerly at the ground.

And Sgt. Jason Carr, standing in the turret of his tank—the turret which he had refused to button up— saw the charging line and listened to the guns spitting out the last of their ammunition, and knew that this was good. For this was the way that cavalry should go —in a surge and with the guidons snapping back in the wind and with the trumpets singing clear in the morning.

He was only vaguely aware of the screaming shell which exploded in front of Tank 2; of the whining

iron which found its mark, for now Sgt. Jason Carr
could hear the roar of other tanks coming in from the
west and he knew that help was here. He felt vaguely
content as the darkness closed around him.

It was a long time before consciousness returned
to him. He was, he knew somehow, lying on the cot
back in the farmhouse and an aidman was bending
over him. There were voices in the kitchen, and he
recognized that of the colonel.

"You people have done a fine job up here, Mulhouse," the colonel was saying. "You bought us the
time that we needed to reorganize. I think that we've
got the Germans on the run now, thanks to you."

That was good, Jason Carr thought fuzzily. That
was what cavalry was for. Footsteps were coming
toward the cot now and the aidman was putting fingers
on his wrist again.

"He's tough, sir," the aidman was saying. "Give him
a few weeks and he'll be as good as new."

Then Eddie Mulhouse was answering, "He's a good
man, corporal. I can't afford to lose him," and Jason
Carr felt warm and good all at once.

Suppose Eddie Mulhouse had been a grease monkey
in a service station before the war? He was a cavalry-
man for all of that. A good cavalryman! Jason turned
his head a little, so that he could see the captain standing there.

"I'll be back, sir," he whispered. Then he remem-

bered what Private Simmons had said yesterday—or
was it the day before yesterday—and his thin lips
quirked a little. "You know, Captain, I rode with
Custer."

# Boys' Life Library Books